Cousins In Action
Operation Golden Llama

Cousins In Action

Operation Golden Llama

* * *

Sam Bond

Cover Art by
Han Randhawa

BOUND PUBLISHING / AUSTIN, TX

Sam Bond/Bound Publishing
P O Box 161081
Austin, TX, 78716
www.CousinsInAction.com

Publisher's Note: This is a work of fiction. Names, characters, places, and
incidents are a product of the author's imagination. Locales and public
names are sometimes used for atmospheric purposes. Any resemblance to
actual people, living or dead, or to businesses, companies, events,
institutions, or locales is completely coincidental.

Illustrations copyright 2013 Han Randhawa
All rights reserved

Book design © 2013, BookDesignTemplates.com

First Edition vs 3.

ISBN 978-0-9911914-1-3

[1. Peru – Fiction. 2. Treasure – Fiction. 3. Cousins – Fiction. 4. Adoption
– Fiction. 5. Incas – Fiction. 6. Travel – Fiction. 7. Spy – Fiction 8.
Adventure – Fiction]

Printed in the United States of America

For Mumpsy

"Life is either a daring adventure or nothing at all." – Helen Keller

treasure [trezh-ure]

1. wealth or riches stashed or accumulated, most likely in the form of precious metals, money or jewels.

2. wealth, rich materials, or valuable objects.

3. anything or person extremely valued or greatly prized: This book was his chief treasure.

S omeone was following her. She'd known they were behind her for at least a mile, but they were getting nearer, bolder. Olivia poked her head out from behind a large leaf and listened. She could hear their breathing, feel their closeness; but the moon was being stubborn, hiding behind a cloud. The night, black as pitch, wasn't overly helpful either.

Behind her a twig snapped, and Olivia felt something warm and sticky dribble down the back of her neck. She sniffed. She didn't want to be judgmental, but whoever was stalking her desperately needed some industrial strength mouthwash.

The moon broke from the clouds. It was now or never. She spun around and smiled. Silhouetted in moonlight Olivia found herself face-to-nose with a llama. She blew out a sigh of relief. A llama she could deal with. She reached up and gave the shaggy beast a pat. It was definitely tempting, but becoming friends with a llama would have to wait 'til she found what she was looking for. You know, if she survived.

Olivia shoved thoughts of a slow, lonely death from her head. She banished thoughts of a quick, brutal death away too. She'd navigated a jungle full of deadly snakes and llama spit. She'd peed in the Peruvian wilds where no eleven-year-old had peed before. *She'd* be fine; it was the others she wasn't sure of.

The shriek of a spider monkey shattered the calm. Olivia sunk to her knees and covered her short, black hair. Pain twisted through her head like an out of control skateboard. Altitude sickness was what the lady had called it. But wasn't she the enemy now? Olivia had trusted her. They all had, and now she was the only one left.

Scrambling to her feet, Olivia laid her head against the long, fluffy neck, stroked the fuzzy nose and, seeing she was running out of time, decided to be brave. She scanned the valley below. They *had* to be here somewhere, but where in the name of Great Aunt Maud were they?

Several miles behind her lay the lost city of the Inca; before her, nothing but dense jungle. Face it, she was stupendously lost. But then, as she turned to swipe the drool off the back of her neck, Olivia saw what she'd been searching for. In the curve of the hillside lay several ragged huts. This had to be the place. With any luck those huts contained her pesky, hair-brained cousins, and if she was really lucky, several billion dollars' worth of treasure.

1

The Secret In The Study

5 days earlier

Grandma Callie lived on a small street, in a boring neighborhood, in the dusty state of Texas. She owned a cat named Chaos, a snake named Hiss and a cactus named Percy. Grandma Callie tried hard to be a normal grandma and, to all outward appearances, she was. She baked delicious apple pies, but served them for breakfast. She sang to her grandchildren, but only in French. She knitted fabulous warm sweaters, but only in lime green and always with a penguin on the back. Try as she might, Grandma Callie was definitely *not* your normal grandma.

Luckily in the Puddleton household eccentricity was an accepted, some might even say encouraged, character flaw. However, in the past few weeks,

Callie Amelia Puddleton had gone from mildly batty to dingbat weird. Everyone agreed, which almost never happened, that something very strange was happening to Grandma. Something secretive. Something mysterious. Something Olivia was determined to discover and would have, if she hadn't fallen off the roof – again.

"Rats!" cried Olivia, as she toppled backwards.

Cagney watched her cousin plunge over the side and snag the roof edge with her fingertips. Olivia hung there, squirming like a week old puppy. As the eldest, Cagney knew she should have undertaken the mission herself, but that would mean climbing onto a dirty roof, and Cagney didn't know any seventh graders who climbed on roofs, fewer still who'd be caught dangling from one.

It was the fourth time this summer the cousins had been dumped at Grandma's and it had taken less than an hour before an experiment involving Chaos, a pot of green paint and a tubby gnome, had seen all five banished to the garden. It had taken a further ten minutes for the cousins to hatch a plan and only seconds more before Olivia was leaping like a demented squirrel (minus fluffy tail) from the sprawling live oak onto Grandma's roof.

Operation Dangle was a simple plan. Climb onto roof, inch across said roof, and dangle precariously off the side in order to see into the study window. It was an unusual plan, and up until recently, one that had been unnecessary. Once upon a time, accessing Grandma's study was simple – encouraged. But, in the last twenty-four hours Grandma had gone to serious trouble to make it impossible. A heavy blind shielding the lower windowpane had been erected and four fat locks were installed on the once welcoming door. Grandma carried so many keys she practically jangled.

Still, Olivia might not have considered sneaking a peak into the study if it hadn't been for three things. Firstly, there was the undeniable fact Grandma didn't want them to, secondly Cagney dared her, and thirdly, and most importantly, there were the phone calls – all three hundred and eleven of them.

With each call the cousins had watched Grandma shuffle towards the study, fumble with the locks and disappear to the sound of a sturdy click. Some of the phone calls took minutes, others so long Olivia wondered if Grandma had keeled over with excitement. When Cagney plucked up courage to ask if everything was okay, Grandma raised her soft, dimpled chin and tapped her nose. Even Olivia agreed, it was hardly a satisfactory answer.

Cagney pushed her glasses upwards and watched as Olivia grappled with gravity. She had briefly suggested her brother undertake the task, but Aidan had never climbed a tree in his life and at the age of eleven there was no way he could be persuaded to embark on such a fool-hardy adventure. Cagney let out a large sigh. "For goodness sake, just let go!"

Aidan peeked over the top of his library book, *Dragons I Have Known and Loved*, and studied his sister's face. "She can't let go, Cagney. She'll break at least a leg, maybe a neck if she's really unlucky. Statistically speaking she has a one in four chance of snapping a major bone. Seeing she's fallen off three times already, this could be it."

Cagney ignored her younger brother. "So? Serves her right. It was a stupid idea."

Lissy glanced up from her laptop. "What do you mean, stupid idea? It was *your* idea."

Cagney shrugged. It might have been her idea, but even *she* was smart enough not to admit it.

Lissy watched her cousin's small body swing to and fro. She grabbed her laptop, scooted off the porch and hurried into the garden. Lissy's laptop was called 'Spider' because she was always on the web. Other children had dogs or cats, but Lissy had Spider and the two were inseparable.

"Olivia, you're a nightmare." Lissy clutched Spider against her sundress. "Grandma will have a fit if you fall again."

Olivia scowled. She had no intention of falling. If she could muscle her way back up and shimmy over three feet she could finally reach her target.

"I'm good," called Olivia, who resembled the pendulum of a clock, trying to swing her legs back onto the roof. "If I could just–"

A roof tile shifted and Olivia's hand gave way. She gasped and her legs flailed as if treading water.

Cagney grabbed her Canon and snapped a picture to commemorate her cousin's short life. "Now you're in trouble."

"Who's in trouble?" Tess stood in the doorway holding a humongous bowl of fruit. She was dressed from head to foot in pink and looked like a Chinese Fancy Nancy.

"Your sister," said Lissy. "She's done it again."

Tess hoisted a smile of watermelon out of the bowl and slurped. Cagney wrenched her eyes away as the juice trickled down Tess' chin onto her sparkly pink tutu. Tess was a walking disaster when it came to food. Cagney couldn't figure out why; it wasn't like she didn't practice enough.

The five cousins had grown up together. Cagney, at twelve, was the oldest. Tess, the youngest, was six, and the three others were squished in the middle. Cagney, Aidan and Lissy all looked similar. They had light hair, pale skin and large hazel eyes. Olivia and Tess looked quite different, having been adopted from China. The one thing the five had in common was their size: they were all tiny.

Tess plunged down the steps and paused under her sister's dangling legs. She shoved the remainder of the watermelon into her mouth and let out a series of incomprehensible squeaks.

Olivia stopped wriggling. "What did she say?"

"I think she's going to catch you," replied Lissy. "But I could be wrong."

Tess flipped her floppy black hair out of her eyes and nodded enthusiastically.

Cagney groaned. "Is she nuts? She'll be squished like a three-day-old salad."

The phone in Grandma's study bleated loudly. Tess gave the end of her nose a good rub. "Grandma's study sure is spooky. Grandma told me a headless ghost lives in the closet."

Cagney slung her camera around her neck and moved towards the house. Shooing Tess away, she stood directly below Olivia and squinted at the flailing feet. "You're crazy. Everyone knows there's no such thing as ghosts."

Aidan reached out and pulled his youngest cousin towards him. "Grandma told me the closet's where she keeps her Barbie collection," he whispered.

Tess boomeranged the watermelon rind into the garden and, grabbing another wedge, slurped down her fifth piece. "Wow!" mumbled Tess. "Barbies? Really? Who knew?"

"Well I know for a fact you're wrong," said Cagney. "The closet's where Grandma keeps Hiss' rats. She lets them run around the study before she puts them in his cage." She drew a finger across her throat dramatically."

"Yuck!" Tess spat out a large watermelon seed. It flew through the air like a rainbow and as if drawn by a magnet landed splat in the middle of Cagney's camera lens.

Afterwards, it was long debated whether Cagney would have heard the cracking wood, the flapping arms, or the sharp intake of breath, if she hadn't been mortified by the seed stuck to the end of her macro lens, but hear it she didn't. And, therefore, unfortunately for Cagney, it was she who broke her cousin's fall.

Landing bottom first on top of Cagney's head may have helped Olivia, but it certainly didn't do much for Cagney.

Olivia checked her limbs for signs of damage and finding none grinned. "Good catch!"

Cagney was about to tell Olivia exactly what she *was* going to do when she caught her, when she realized what was wrong. Gingerly she patted the surrounding area.

"Is this what you're looking for?" Tess picked up a mangled frame and pushed it into her cousin's outstretched hand. Cagney snatched the crumpled mess, and with as much dignity as she could muster, rested the splintered glasses onto her nose.

Unfortunately, it was then she saw the blood. Letting out a small squeak Cagney raised her hand and watched a thick red line trickle along her arm. Olivia squatted down, grabbed the edge of her tee and gave Cagney's arm a cursory swipe. "You're good! Doesn't even need stitches. Barely any. At least, not as many as last time."

Cagney flicked her frizzy hair off her face. She opened her mouth but Aidan cut her off. Whatever was going to come out of Cagney's mouth was definitely not something Tess should hear.

Aidan swallowed hard and tried to look at anything other than the blood. "So, what *does* Grandma keep in her study?"

"I'm rooting for the Barbies," said Tess, "with pink puffy tutus."

Olivia stepped over Cagney's body and pushed her nose up against the heavily veiled window. "Well, whatever it is, Grandma obviously doesn't want us to find out."

Suddenly, the porch door creaked open. The outline of a small, angular woman was silhouetted in the doorframe. With a scowl on her face and a green cat wedged securely beneath her arm, Grandma Callie stood in the doorway, and she didn't look happy.

*
*
*
*

2

The Mysterious Pet Sitter

Lissy zipped her suitcase and tossed it towards the door. "I still can't believe Grandma's taking us on vacation … and to Peru."

Tess bounded onto her bed. "I bet she's so excited taking all five of us."

"She didn't look very excited," said Aidan.

Olivia grinned. She ran a hand over the snoozing snake curled like a pinwheel on her bed. "I've seen meat loaf more excited than Grandma, right Hiss?" Hiss opened an eye at the sound of his name and his tongue darted out.

"It's hard to tell with Grandma. She's not exactly the excitable type." Lissy raised an eyebrow. "Well, unless you draw toadstools all over her Gardens of England calendar," she added, looking at Olivia.

Grandma Callie was originally from England and her entire house was littered with trinkets reminding her of home. From framed pictures of the Tower of London to a scaled model of Stonehenge, Grandma's living room was a walking advertisement for the Britain she still considered great.

Olivia's dimple deepened. "Yep! She got pretty excited about that."

Cagney surveyed the fifteen piles of clothes laid neatly in front of her. "I'm guessing this is not Grandma's dream vacation."

Olivia drummed her fingers on the bedspread. "Ya think? She's had a face like a smacked bottom ever since she told us."

"Does anyone know *why* she's going to Peru?" asked Lissy. "Doesn't it seem slightly out of character? I mean, it's not like she's ever gone anywhere before."

Aidan glanced up from his library book. "I guess that's what happens when you get a gazillion phone calls – and before you can say "lolloping llamas" we're off."

"Something's off." Olivia's forehead furrowed. "And I intend to find out what."

It was twenty-four hours since Grandma Callie received the last of her 312 phone calls and since then the cousins had barely seen her. Within an hour, Grandma's next-door neighbor, Mrs. Snoops, had arrived to take the cousins shopping.

Mrs. Snoops, much to Aidan's disgust, was normally only viewed across the garden fence while hanging out her incredibly large underwear. Needless to say, she was not the cousins' favorite person in the world. When Olivia told her they didn't need new clothes Mrs. Snoops explained that although it was summer in Texas, in South America it was winter.

Each cousin bought clothes essential to them. Olivia chose sweatpants. Lissy, wool dresses. And Tess! Tess chose clothes in varying shades of pink, plus a warm cerise poncho. Cagney crammed shut the lid of her suitcase and plopped on top trying to make both ends meet. The bag, resembling an overstuffed sandwich, was not cooperating. Puffing with exertion Cagney slid her duct-taped glasses back up her nose and sunk to the floor.

Olivia scooped up her jumble of clothes and squeezed them into a battered backpack. Adding her Red Sox cap, she zipped it, chucked it in the general direction of the door and slouched onto her bed. Cagney was now standing on top of her case doing some sort of dance. Olivia did not understand how a few days in Peru could warrant quite so many clothes; then again, Olivia was not your typical girl.

"I've never been to South America," said Cagney, who had finally persuaded her suitcase to behave.

Olivia watched Hiss uncurl and slither across her legs. "You've never been to South Anywhere. None of us have."

"The only place Grandma ever took me was the library." Lissy winced at the memory. "She gave me a book on toads and left me there for three hours."

"She took *us* to the grocery store and left us in the bakery." Olivia grinned. "By the time she got back Tess had eaten twenty dollars' worth of muffins."

Lissy looked concerned. "You don't think she'd abandon us in South America, do you?"

Aidan snapped his book shut. "Of course she wouldn't."

Lissy caught Aidan's eye.

"Nah!" they said together, "she wouldn't."

Olivia ran her fingers down Hiss, who had curled into her lap. "This is going to be the coolest vacation ever."

Tess seized her wand and spun on tiptoe. "Yep, my pink fluffy tutu is just quivering with excitement. That's always a good sign, right Olivia?"

Olivia was prone to deafness where her younger sister was concerned and ignored the question.

"I hope we go to Machu Picchu," said Lissy, tapping away at Spider.

"Machu whatchu?" asked Olivia.

"Machu Picchu. Spider says it's an ancient city perched on top of a mountain. Here, take a look."

Lissy spun Spider around on the bed and Aidan's jaw dropped. "Wow! That's ... that's ... well that's pretty darn cool, isn't it? Do people live there?"

Lissy shook her head. "Nope. It was abandoned, forgotten. It lay undiscovered in the jungle for hundreds of years."

Cagney rolled her eyes. "Fascinating – no honestly it's just fab–"

Lissy grabbed her pillow and aimed it at Cagney. It was a regular occurrence. Cagney had about as much interest in anything Spider said as she did long division. Lissy, always eager for knowledge, could not bear to be teased.

A loud knock at the front door made Lissy pause mid-throw as she heard Grandma Callie's fluffy slippers shuffling down the hallway. The cousins fell silent as they listened to an unfamiliar voice.

Lissy looked puzzled. "Who do you think it is?"

Tess stopped bouncing on her bed and listened. "Maybe it's Mrs. Snoops."

Olivia frowned. "That's never Mrs. Snoops."

"Maybe she got a cold and her voice went down several octaves," suggested Aidan.

Footsteps stormed down the hallway and without warning the bedroom door burst open. Filling the doorway was a man so large he was almost rectangular. He wore a black sweater, black pants and black glasses. His face, the color of night, had a long scar across one cheek. Under one arm he held Chaos, in the other, a cage of rats. All of them looked like they would rather be somewhere else – especially the rats.

Tess' eyes bulged. "Nope, that's not Mrs. Snoops."

"Yo!" The man's voice was a deep baritone.

The cousins were not easily intimidated, but the man was huge. If Tess had known what the word ominous meant, she would have used it. As the oldest, Cagney was always the spokesperson. Today, she would eagerly have given up this self-appointed honor. She cleared her throat. "Er … can we help you?"

The stranger scanned the room. Aidan had the distinct impression that behind the glasses he was absorbing every last detail. When he got to Olivia he stopped. He stepped forward, reaching her in two strides. He stared over the top of his glasses and into her dark, almond eyes. "I've come to collect the, erm, snake."

Olivia stopped tickling the large boa constrictor and swallowed. "What for?" Her voice came out as a squeak and she blushed at the weakness.

The man took a final step towards her, his shadow falling across her face. "I'm … er … I'm … I'm going to look after him while your grandma's out of town."

Tess bounced off the bed and landed squarely between the man and her sister. She reached approximately his navel and, gazing up at his face, gave him a toothless grin. "You're the pet sitter, right?"

Lissy hid her smile. That was the thing about Tess; she always thought the best of strangers, even when the stranger looked like they could pluck her up by the tutu and fling her out the window.

"Someding like that," the man sniffed.

Tess grabbed a box of tissues and held them up. "Do you need a Kleenex?"

"Dno," snuffled the man, stifling a sneeze. "I'm fine. But I fink I'm allergic to cats."

Tess smiled. "Yep, the green ones are always the worst, but everyone says it'll fade in time!"

Olivia grasped Hiss around his belly and slipped off her bed. Even though Olivia was five years older than Tess, she was only marginally taller and the man towered above her. He crouched, and on tiptoes she placed Hiss around the stranger's neck.

"Dhanks," said the pet sitter as he turned and with three long strides was out the door.

The room suddenly felt a lot larger.

The front door slammed and Lissy let out a breath she didn't know she was holding. "I've never heard of a pet sitter being allergic to cats before."

Aidan added his library book to his backpack and zipped it shut. "Yeah, I don't believe he was a pet sitter at all."

Olivia crossed to the window and watched her beloved Hiss head down the garden path. "Whoever heard of a pet sitter wearing all black?"

Cagney joined her. They watched the pet sitter toss the rats into the back of a long black car. "I agree. That sweater was cashmere and *everyone* knows cashmere and cat hair just don't mix."

*

* *

3

Limas and Llamas and Bears – Oh My!

Cagney's head bobbed up from the seat in front. "What are you reading?"

Aidan grinned. "*Spanish for the Seriously Stupid.*"

"Why aren't you learning Peruvian?" asked Tess.

"Most people speak Spanish in Peru," Aidan explained.

Tess squished her nose against the airplane window. "Does it tell you where Peruvia is?"

Aidan smiled. "It's on the South American coast."

"To be specific, Spider says Ecuador and Colombia are north, Brazil's east and Bolivia and Chile are south," said Lissy.

Cagney rolled her eyes. "Good grief. It's like traveling with my very own Encyclopedia Britannica."

Tess counted off the map directions on her fingers. "What about west?"

"The Pacific Ocean," the others chimed together.

"It's a crazy long way," said Lissy. "Once we land in Lima we'll have flown over 3,000 miles."

"You don't say!" Cagney snapped a sleep mask with the words 'wake me and I'll bite you' over her eyes and folded her arms.

"I thought a lima was an animal," said Tess.

"You're thinking of a lemur," said Aidan. "You know, big eyes, cute ears, lives in Madagascar."

"So what are those animals that look like sheep with long necks?" asked Tess.

"Llamas," said Lissy.

"I've always wanted a pet llama," said Olivia. "I could ride her to school."

Olivia was known for her love of animals. She thought taking care of pets should make up for getting C's in math – unfortunately her parents did not.

"Aaaah, a pet llama," said Tess. "I would call her Cuddles, right Olivia?"

Lissy smiled. "You might see one. Llamas are indigenous to South America."

"What does 'indigenous' mean?" asked Tess.

Tess had been taught that there were no dumb questions. Much to the irritation of her entire family, she took full advantage of this.

"It means they're native to Peru. They weren't brought there from somewhere else," explained Aidan.

"Actually, llamas are quite interesting." Lissy angled the picture on Spider towards Tess. "They can grow up to six feet and spit up to eight."

"Gross," muttered Cagney.

Lissy ignored her cousin. "They're pack animals and one of the most sure-footed animals in the world."

Tess emptied a pack of peanuts into her mouth. "What does 'sure-footed' mean?" she mumbled, bits of peanuts spraying out the sides of her mouth.

Lissy edged Spider away from the flying debris. "It means they won't fall over, even if they're running down the side of a mountain. People keep them for their wool, which is really soft, or their meat."

Cagney snatched off her sleep mask and flung herself around. "You mean people eat them?"

Tess shook her head. "Poor Cuddles."

"Hey, Olivia. Spider says you *could* ride Cuddles to school. Children can easily ride a llama, but if an adult tries, the llama will lie down and squish them."

"You know, Lissy, you're way too smart for a ten-year-old," said Tess, munching on a donut.

"Comes from being an only child," said Aidan, who had only dreamed of such joy. The airplane's nose dropped, and Aidan gasped.

"I'm so excited," said Tess. "Only a triple banana split with extra cherries would make life more perfect."

Cagney pointed at the brown stain spread across the front of Tess' pink fluffy dress. "Didn't you inhale, I mean enjoy, one of those in Houston?"

"I might have!" Tess pulled out a pink polka-dotted handkerchief the size of Spain and started to dab at her dress.

Cagney shook her head. She wasn't sure what she'd done in a previous life to deserve her current situation but, whatever it was, she was paying for it now.

Cagney surveyed the plane, the passengers and finally the air steward heading in their direction. The air steward was tall, slim and wore a look that Cagney so often associated with adults.

The air steward drew level and stopped. He attempted a smile, but failed. "Are you traveling alone?" he asked.

"No, sir. Our Grandma's with us. But she was bumped to first class," replied Lissy.

Cagney scowled. "I don't know why we couldn't sit there too. It's not like we're loud or anything."

The air steward observed the cousins. The small Chinese child was pouring lemonade down her dress. The girl with the laptop was pulling peanuts out of her curls and the boy looked like he was going to be sick.

"It's a crying shame," he commented.

Tess stuffed the last of her donut in her mouth and licked her lips. "I can't imagine why she doesn't want to be at the back of the plane with us. It's great being next to the bathroom. Plus you feel every bump; it's like being on a really dangerous roller coaster."

Aidan let out a small moan. He gripped his stomach and shut his eyes. Aidan got motion sickness in hammocks. Once he'd thrown up on a paddleboat in the middle of a pond. Aidan did not want to be reminded of roller coasters. Aidan wanted to be reminded of flat Texas land, preferably with a few cows. Cows that did not sway, bump or smell of donuts.

The air steward reached into the seat back pocket and slapped a vomitus green bag into Aidan's hands. "And she's going to meet you at the gate?"

"Yes, sir." Cagney peered at the steward through her duct-taped glasses. "Our grandma likes us to be independent. She says we're very capable. As I like to say, everyman for herself."

Lissy laid her head back and smiled. Cagney was always getting her sayings muddled up; it was one of her more endearing qualities.

"What do you mean independent?" asked Olivia, as the steward hustled back up the aisle. "We've never been anywhere by ourselves."

Cagney started shoving copies of *Vogue* into her carry-on. "But it makes us sound so international. You don't want them to think we've never left Texas, do you?"

"I don't care what they think. As long as they land this plane in one piece," said Aidan, who was turning a rather delicate shade of green.

"Stuff your head between your legs," Olivia suggested, as they bumped towards the ground and into their first adventure.

4

Abandoned

The cousins successfully negotiated both customs and immigration and stood in the cavernous terminal, waiting.

Tess looked around the crowded airport, crossed her legs and did a jig. "I need to go potty."

Cagney pushed her battered glasses onto the bridge of her nose, and with great effort withheld the first thought that came to mind. "You should have gone on the plane."

Tess jigged faster. "I *did* go on the plane."

Olivia gave her sister a withering look. "Then you shouldn't have drunk fifteen glasses of pink lemonade."

Tess grimaced. "You have a point."

Lissy glanced towards Grandma. She was busy chatting with an official-looking man. "We should all go while Grandma's dealing with that guy in the uniform. Aidan, can you stay with the bags?"

Aidan raised his chin and stuck out his chest. "Yep! Unlike you women, we men have bladders of steel."

"Absolutely!" Olivia shook her head. "Bladders of steel, stomachs of cotton candy."

Aidan looked down sheepishly. The landing 30 minutes ago had not been one of his finer moments.

Cagney shook her head and followed her cousins to the restroom. "Sometimes I can't believe I'm related to him."

"Yeah." Olivia watched Tess do a Tigger impression as she bounced ahead down the corridor. "Sometimes it's definitely a relief to have been adopted."

Ten minutes later the girls emerged from the bathroom. Aidan stood guarding the bags; the green tinge, that previously consumed his face, now replaced with a look of panic.

Lissy rushed towards him. "What's wrong?"

"It's Grandma," said Aidan. "She's gone."

"What do you mean gone?" exclaimed Olivia.

Cagney folded her arms and stuck out a hip. "Obviously there's a simple explanation."

"She probably went to the bathroom, right Aidan?" said Tess.

"Maybe. If the bathroom's through those doors marked 'Security'." Aidan pointed across the terminal.

Lissy sunk to the floor. Tired and flustered she leaned against her suitcase. "But she can't have left us."

Aidan bit his lip. "Not so much left as taken away."

"What do you mean taken away?" asked Olivia.

"Well, that's the weird thing," said Aidan. "It sounds kind of strange, but … the person who took her away … well, he kind of looked like the pet sitter. You know, but without a green cat under his arm."

Tess plopped onto the floor next to Lissy. "Really? The pet sitter's in Lima?"

"Of course not," said Cagney. "Aidan has an overly developed imagination. Aidan, tell Tess about your overly developed imagination."

Aidan scratched his head. "But honestly. He looked just like him."

"Did she tell us to wait for her?" asked Lissy.

Aidan shook his head.

Tess sprang to her feet. "Maybe by the time we get something to eat, she'll be back."

"Maybe by the time she returns you'll have run up a tab even Grandma can't pay for," said Cagney.

"*Au contraire.*" Aidan brightened. "Money is *not* our problem."

"Oh con what?" asked Olivia.

Lissy's small voice floated up from the floor. "It means 'not at all'."

Cagney changed hips and spun to face Aidan. "What do you mean it's not our problem? Money does not grow on thieves, you know."

Aidan fished in his pocket, drew out a huge wad of neatly folded bills and fanned them in Cagney's face.

"Sweet!" said Olivia.

"Yep. Grandma left us loaded."

"But it still doesn't help us know what to do." Lissy did not like out of control situations and, in her mind, being stranded in a foreign airport in South America definitely came under the heading of out of control.

"Oh, yeah, I forgot." Aidan stuffed the money into his pocket. "We're supposed to go through those doors, and look for someone called Lucila. Apparently she's very reliable."

Olivia gave Aidan a high-five. "Excellent."

Aidan pulled Lissy to her feet and gave her a squeeze. "Come on worrywart. We'll be fine."

"Honestly, Lissy, how hard can it be?" said Olivia. "It'll be an adventure."

Lissy shook her head. Olivia was always looking for adventure; the problem with Olivia's adventures was they frequently went wrong – horribly wrong. "But our parents would have a fit if they knew."

Olivia slung her backpack over her shoulder and marched across the terminal. "Good thing they don't then."

The cousins followed Olivia towards the doors Aidan had pointed to. Throwing them open they were assaulted with a noise unlike anything they'd ever heard. Lissy's eyes opened wide. The airport was crowded with brightly dressed people. Women with long braids spilling down their backs and wearing strange Frisbee-like hats stood at the barrier. Men with brightly colored ponchos stood in groups. The airport even smelled different.

An exotic smell, thought Cagney.

The smell of excitement, thought Olivia.

The smell of food, thought Tess.

Lissy shuffled along hugging Spider to her chest and grumbling. "How hard can it be, she says ... there are hundreds of people here ... we're never going to find *anyone* in this crowd." *Honestly, grown-ups could be so unreliable.*

Tess pointed at someone dressed in an elaborately decorated poncho. "*She* looks like a Lucila."

Olivia shook her head. "I don't think so."

"It *might* be," said Tess.

"Only if Lucila's a man," replied Olivia.

Tess tilted her head to the left and studied the man. "Wow! The men sure dress colorful over here."

"How about over there," said Aidan.

Lissy spun around. "Which one?"

Aidan pointed. "The one with the sign that says Callie Puddleton."

Olivia nodded. "That would definitely be my choice."

5

Watch Out!

The sign was so large that the person behind it could barely be seen. Except for a cherry red pair of boots sticking out the bottom, the person was invisible.

Cagney approached the boots. "Excuse me, but could you possibly be Lucila?"

"*Si,*" came the voice from the behind the sign. "And you must be the leetle Puddletons." The sign was tossed to one side revealing a plump woman with a crinkled face and large crooked smile.

"Welcome to Lima, my amigos." She ruffled Tess' long black hair and beamed at the cousins. Let me see now, you must be the Tess, the Lissy and the Cagney." She glanced over at Aidan and Olivia.

"And here we have the two boys, Aidan and Oliver, right?"

Olivia grinned. She was never happier than when mistaken for a boy. With her cropped black hair and distinct lack of girl's clothing, this happened on a regular basis. It had been a long time since she or her cousins had bothered to correct anyone's mistake.

Cagney stared at the strange looking woman and wondered if gold teeth were a sign of prosperity in Peru.

Pulling herself together, Cagney remembered her manners and tore her eyes away from Lucila's twinkling smile. "I'm sorry, but our grandma's been delayed. She said you'd take care of us?"

Lucila slapped Cagney on the back. Cagney shot forward from the force, but Lucila didn't seem to notice. Linking arms with Tess on one side and Lissy on the other, she motioned for the others to follow. "Thees is not a problem. Come. I will take the good care of you. Your grandma and I are great friends; I have a feeling we will become friends too. No?"

Lucila led the cousins out of the airport and into the night. After several wrong turns, and a trek through a passageway Cagney vowed she would never forget, they finally arrived at their destination.

"Here." Lucila fumbled in her pockets and triumphantly brought out a set of keys. "This is our ride."

"Whoa!" Aidan's eyes widened.

Tess rubbed the end of her nose. "That's different."

Cagney snapped a picture. "Does it have seatbelts?"

Olivia stared open-mouthed. Spotlighted under a fluorescent light was an open-top jeep that had once been blue. Now it was hard to tell, as the blue had become an ocean decorated with plastic marine life. Fish, sharks, octopuses, and even a few ducks were glued over every inch.

Olivia swung her legs over the side and tumbled into the back. "This is the type of car you're not going to lose in a parking lot."

"This is *my* type of 'mobile'," said Tess. "When I'm older, I want to have one just like it – but in pink."

Lucila jumped behind the steering wheel and revved the engine. Salsa music blared from the radio.

Tess sashayed towards the front seat. "Oh! Me likey," said Tess, swishing her dress in time to the samba.

Cagney rolled her eyes. To think, she could be in Texas getting a pedicure. Instead she was in a rolling aquarium with dubious seatbelts, no air conditioning and headed lord knows where.

"Ready?" asked Lucila.

But before anyone had a chance to reply, Lucila put her foot to the floor and the jeep took off like a missile. The cousins' heads slammed backwards as Lucila tore down the ramp and into the city.

The cousins squinted at sights hurtling by, lost in their own thoughts. Olivia wondered if she would ever own such a cool car. Lissy wondered if Lucila had ever hit anyone and Aidan eyed Cagney's overstuffed bag as his best option for when the time came to throw up.

"What time do the shops close?" asked Cagney, spying some really cool stores.

"The shops stay open very late, but in the afternoon we *siesta*."

"*Siesta?*" Spanish had never been Cagney's favorite subject. She was beginning to wish she'd paid more attention.

"We nap," explained Lucila. "Then we are fresh, like daisies, for the rest of the day."

Lucila swerved in and out of traffic ignoring horns, gesturing wildly, barreling through streets alive with people.

"How many people live in Lima?" asked Aidan.

Lucila scooted around and smiled. "Almost eight million. It is the capital of Peru and very busy. Lots of people come from the country to try and make the money. We are a very friendly city."

Lissy gasped and jabbed her finger toward the windshield. "Excuse me ... Ms. Lucila, ma'am ... there's a ... um."

Cagney lowered her camera and instantly saw what Lissy was looking at. At the bottom of a hill a restaurant had just closed and a gaggle of teenagers were spilling into the street. Lucila saw them at the same time. She slammed on the brakes, but the jeep continued downwards. Oblivious to the screeching tires, the teenagers stood laughing bang smack in the middle of the road.

Cagney hid behind Olivia. "I'm too young to die."

Olivia shoved Cagney back into her seat. "Get a grip woman. And what do you mean you're too young – you're the oldest!"

"Move!" Tess lurched forward and waved both arms in the air. "You'll be squished like bugs."

Careening down the hill in the fearless jeep, the cousins braced for impact. At the last second, the jeep juddered to a stop. Bursting from her seat Lucila released a stream of jumbled Spanish. Cagney, gaping at the steam rising from the tires, made a mental note never to complain about their family minivan again.

Olivia glanced at Aidan and nodded toward Lucila. "Do you know what she's saying?"

Aidan raised his eyebrows, wiped his brow and grinned. "I'm getting the general idea."

Laughing and waving, the teenagers ambled onto the sidewalk. Lucila sank into her seat and clapped her hands together. "See," she said with a broad smile, "Lima very friendly place."

6

The Angry Man

The rest of the journey was uneventful. Lucila twisted her way through the streets of Lima – each one seeming to get narrower and more deserted. Without warning Lucila hit the curb and lurched to a stop. She leapt from her seat and grabbing the cousins' bags started tossing them onto the sidewalk.

The cousins tumbled out the jeep and stared. Standing in front of them was a rickety old hotel with a large double door and several dusty windows. A neon sign flickered from the rooftop announcing the presence of OTEL MISERI.

Lissy gulped. "This is where we're staying?"

"*Si, si*," said Lucila, sending another bag flying into the air.

"Are you sure this is the right place?" asked Cagney.

"Quite sure," said Lucila. "This is where your grandma always stays."

"When Grandma went to Branson she stayed at the Marriott," said Aidan.

"This is definitely no Marriott," said Tess.

"This is definitely no Branson," said Olivia, ducking as Cagney's suitcase flew towards her.

"Grandma's been here before?" Lissy was shocked at the thought of Grandma staying in such a place.

Lucila fished out the remaining bag and launched it towards Lissy. "Of course. Why, she and I go back many years."

"You do?" Olivia looked Lucila up and down. Lucila didn't look like anyone their grandma knew. Grandma's friends looked like Mrs. Snoops. They had nice perms and wore several layers of beige. Lucila didn't have on any clothing that could be considered anywhere close to beige. From her large hooped earrings to her long flowing skirt, she looked way too fun to be friends with Grandma.

Lucila angled herself back behind the wheel. "Have fun leetle Puddletons," and she zoomed away leaving the cousins alone on the grimy street.

Cagney looked at Aidan accusingly. "Great! Just great. *This* is a disaster."

Lissy stared down the dark alleyway. "What do we do now?"

At once the doors to the crumbling building swung open. Silhouetted in the doorframe stood a man who filled most of it. Sporting a well-cut suit and a mass of black curls he lurched towards the cousins, his face breaking into an ample smile.

"*Puddelitos!*" he cried, opening his arms wide, greeting each of them with a viselike hug. "Señor Gustavo welcomes the grandchildren of the fabulous Callie Puddleton to Hotel Miserias."

Aidan peered around the deserted alley. "Who's Señor Gustavo?"

"Who's Señor Gustavo?" The man looked hurt. "Why *this* is a Señor Gustavo," he said, stabbing a large sausage-like finger at his chest. "Your grandmother never mentioned me?"

"It seems Grandma never mentioned a lot of things," said Olivia.

The cousins followed Señor Gustavo through the peeling wooden doors. The inside of Hotel Miserias looked like the set of a 1950's horror movie. Tess edged closer to Aidan and slipped her hand into his. To the right was a sweep of stairs, to the left a pair of French doors. Nestled below the curve of the staircase, illuminated by a single light bulb, stood the reception desk. The cousins inched across the cracked terracotta tile and dumped their bags in a pile.

Lissy glanced around anxiously. "Sir, is our grandma here?"

Señor Gustavo sucked in his belly and wedged himself behind the front desk. He turned to face the five, a large beaming smile lighting his face. Olivia thought she had never seen anyone quite so pleased to see them. She was beginning to like Señor Gustavo.

"Do not worry. Your grandma will show up in a couple of days. She has people to see, places to go, parties to attend."

"Parties!" Cagney's eyes opened wide. "She's gone to a party without me?"

"Who knows?" Señor Gustavo waved his arms around his head. "It is nothing to worry about. Señora Puddleton knows we will take a good care of you. We are like family."

"We are?" asked Olivia.

"We are," Señor Gustavo assured her.

Cagney eyed the peeling paintwork. "How fun!"

If Señor Gustavo caught the edge in Cagney's voice he certainly was too polite to show it. Lissy thought he might well be the most enthusiastic person she'd ever met – well, apart from Tess.

Señor Gustavo turned his attention to Lissy and bowed low, his hand flourished behind him; his nose almost touched the desk. "Señor Gustavo is going to give you his largest and best suite. It is where your Grandma always stays. Your Grandma is very particular to a south-facing room."

Lissy was not sure whether she should bow in return and so bobbed a curtsy instead. "Thank you so much."

Señor Gustavo raised himself to his full height; his eyes twinkled with a smile. "Think nothing of it; it is Señor Gustavo's pleasure."

Lissy unclenched her fingers and allowed her shoulders to sink past her ears. Señor Gustavo collected a key from behind the desk and handed it to her.

"Now, if you would be so kind as to sign the guest book." Señor Gustavo pushed the book towards Aidan.

"Señor Aidan would be delighted," said Aidan, with an air of importance.

The grin was quickly wiped off his face by Cagney stomping on his foot.

"Yowza!" yelped Aidan.

"If there is anything you need, anything at all, Señor Gustavo will be at your service."

The cousins grabbed their bags and trudged up the wooden staircase. Halfway up the stairs the front door crashed open with a bang. The cousins spun around. In the doorway stood a tall, skinny man, with a shock of blond hair and a small pair of glasses on the end of his nose. He strode to the front desk and flung down his backpack.

Señor Gustavo took a hasty step backwards "*Buenos noches,*" he said, with a nervous bow.

The blond man leaned forward. His voice was raspy with anger. "Gabriela?" he croaked.

Hearing footsteps behind them Lissy turned to see a young woman hurrying down the stairs.

"*Con permiso,*" she whispered as she brushed past them.

The dark-haired woman rushed across the lobby and approached the angry man.

"Pietro," she said in a soft voice.

The man swung around, his pink face flushed and menacing. The woman took his arm. Pulling him through the lobby, they disappeared through the French doors, into a dimly lit courtyard. The door slammed behind them and Señor Gustavo and Lissy's shoulders lowered simultaneously. Wiping his forehead, Señor Gustavo puffed a sigh of relief.

Cagney raised her eyebrows and sniffed. "I wonder what that was about?"

Olivia was already bounding onto the landing. "It's none of *our* business. Come on."

By the time the others reached the top of the staircase Olivia was halfway along the hallway. The corridor was dark; the wallpaper was peeling and the whole place smelled like boiled cabbage. At the very end, Olivia found room number 24. She gave the door a sharp push. An eerie creek echoed along the hall reminding Olivia of Halloween. The cousins poured into the room and the door shut behind them with a click. There was silence. The cousins stood in total darkness.

"Ermm! Light switch anyone?" suggested Lissy.

It was probably as well no one could see what anyone else was doing. Aidan promptly walked into the bathroom and almost fell into the toilet. Olivia resembled Frankenstein as she stumbled around the room, and Cagney sunk onto the uneven wood floor and waited.

Lissy clutched Spider to her chest and decided the best thing to do was find a wall. Where there was a wall there would be a light switch.

"Found it," yelled Aidan.

A whirring noise filled the room.

"Doofus!" said Olivia. "That's the fan."

The cousins continued to fumble.

"Hey!" yelled Cagney. "That's not the light switch."

"Are you sure?" asked Tess.

Cagney batted Tess' hand away. "Positive," she answered, sniffing indignantly. "That's my nose."

Finally the cousins heard a click and the room filled with light. They gazed around the old fashioned room: three four-poster beds covered with thick red blankets dominated it. Two doors led from the room: one to the bathroom, the other to an ornate balcony. One large armoire, a dresser and a chair fit for a king completed the ensemble.

Lissy lunged towards the nearest bed. "I'm really starting to like this traveling thing."

"Me too," Tess said, sleepily.

And quickly and quietly, all five snuck under the beautiful woven blankets and fell fast asleep.

7

Breakfast with Gabriela

The cousins woke bright-eyed and hungry. Sitting in the courtyard, they happily devoured fried sweet potatoes and slurped hot chocolate.

"Don't look now," said Aidan, "but there's the lady from last night."

Cagney turned to face the dark-haired woman sitting in the corner. The woman glanced over and waved. Cagney huffed. "Great, now she thinks we're staring at her."

"We are staring at her," said Lissy.

"Oh the poor thing," said Tess. "She's sitting all alone."

"So?" said Cagney.

"But food *never* tastes as good when you're alone. Donuts are definitely scrummier if eaten with company, and scrummelicious if eaten outdoors." Tess took a huge slurp of hot chocolate. She clattered the large oval cup onto the table and licked her lips. A large blob of whipped cream perched on the end of her button nose. "I vote we ask her to join us."

Cagney took a deep breath. "Are you nuts?" She stopped. "Okay, forget that question. But I totally forbid you to invite a complete stranger to join us."

Olivia raised her eyebrows. "Yeah, Cagney. She could be a mass murderer lurking in South American hotel courtyards, just waiting to lure unchaperoned children into her lair."

Cagney nodded. "Exactly! We should mind our own business."

"Well it's too late now." Aidan smoothed down his shirt and sat up straight. "She's heading this way."

"What?" Cagney turned to see the young woman crossing the courtyard. She snatched her latest copy of *Vogue* off the table and hid inside it. Seconds later the magazine was lifted from her hands, flipped the right way, and handed back to her.

"I always find it much easier to see what the clothes look like if the magazine is facing the right way," said a lilting voice.

Cagney blushed and peered into the velvety eyes of possibly the most beautiful woman she had ever seen. She was nothing less than stunning. Wearing khakis and a sweater, her mocha skin was free of make-up and her long thick hair was pulled into a ponytail.

"*Hola.*" A broad and welcoming smile spread across the woman's face, a smile Cagney could not help but return.

Aidan cleared his throat. "Er, hello!" His voice came out as a squeak.

"I do not think we have been introduced." She extended her hand and Aidan quickly wiped sweet potato on the checkered tablecloth before clasping it.

"My name is Gabriela. May I?" She pointed at a spare chair.

Aidan jumped up and pulled out the chair.

Gabriela smiled. "A gentleman. So rare these days."

Aidan went scarlet. Cagney pulled herself together and lowered her magazine. "It's very nice to meet you. I'm Cagney, and this is my brother, Aidan, and our cousins Olivia, Lissy and Tess Puddleton."

"Puddleton?" Gabriela glanced down and bit her lip. A look of concern fluttered across her pretty face. A second later it was gone. She pasted on a smile and looked up. "That is a *very* unusual name."

"Tell me about it," said Olivia.

"And you are here … with your parents?"

"We're with our grandma, ma'am," said Lissy. "But she's kinda missing."

"Oh!" Gabriela frowned. "I am dreadfully sorry to hear that."

"Don't worry," said Tess. "We're doing really great. We found breakfast all by ourselves."

Gabriela leaned over and wiped the smudge of cream off Tess' nose. "So I see."

"Besides, Grandma always shows up in the end." Lissy frowned. "At least I hope she does."

Gabriela turned toward Lissy and gave her a reassuring smile.

"It's a habit of hers." Aidan had finally resumed his normal color. "You know what grandmas can be like."

Gabriela looked confused. "A habit?"

"Forgetting us," explained Lissy.

Olivia circled her index finger next to her ear. "She's a bit scatter-brained."

Gabriela smothered a smile. "Obviously."

Tess shoveled the last sweet potato into her mouth and wiped orange mush off her ears. "Are you a model?"

"Oh no." Gabriela laughed. "I am a fashion photographer."

Cagney's prized copy of *Vogue* slid to the floor. "Really? I'm a photographer too."

"Then you will have to show me your work," said Gabriela.

Nobody other than Cagney's parents had ever asked to see her pictures before. Cagney beamed. "Really? I'd love that."

"Are you staying long?" asked Gabriela.

"At least 'til Grandma arrives," said Lissy. "Then we don't know what we're doing."

"How exciting. It sounds like you cousins are having a real adventure."

The door to the courtyard flew open and Gabriela glanced up. At once her face changed. Tess turned to see the blond man staring right at them. Glaring, he beckoned Gabriela towards him.

"Pietro: he's your boyfriend, right?" asked Tess.

"Something like that." Gabriela glanced down nervously. Her hands were shaking. She quickly shoved them under the tablecloth. "I am very sorry, but I have to go. If your grandma arrives, please let me know; I would love to meet her."

Gabriela scraped back her wicker chair and hurried across the courtyard. Pietro bent to whisper something in her ear. Gabriela shook her head and left. Pietro gave the cousins one last sneer and followed her.

The five were silent. It was troubling – very troubling.

Finally Cagney broke the silence. "Did you see Gabriela's face when she saw him?"

"Yes," whispered Lissy. "She was scared."

"I don't get this moody Latin thing," said Tess.

"He's not even Latin," said Cagney.

Tess looked puzzled. "He isn't?"

"I doubt it," said Cagney. "How many blond South American men do you know?"

Tess frowned. "Well, so far I've only met Señor Gustavo, and I've a feeling that's a wig."

Across the courtyard came a friendly voice. "*Hola!*"

Lissy spun around. "Lucila!" Lissy had never been happier to see anyone. It was all well and good finding breakfast by themselves, but what next? Lucila might be a trifle eccentric, but at least she was a native eccentric.

"Hello leetle Puddletons." Lucila bobbed across the courtyard to greet them. "I hope you sleep well in The City of Kings."

Tess grinned. "Like a queen."

"Are you ready to discover Lima?" asked Lucila.

Lissy brightened. A flood of relief swept her body. They weren't to be left to fend for themselves.

It seemed there was a plan. Lissy smiled. Plans were good.

"I just need to get my camera." Cagney pushed back her chair and headed across the courtyard.

"And my Spanish book." Aidan followed her.

"And my pink striped umbrella," said Tess, rising.

"Your umbrella?" asked Lucila. "But it is not going to rain."

Tess tipped back her chin and squinted at the sky. "But it's so cloudy."

Lucila flashed Tess a large, gold smile. "Fog. In the winter Lima gets the fog."

Lissy peered at the grey above. "You're sure it's not going to rain?"

"Quite sure. In the summer we have the nice blue skies and the warm weather. But in the winter we get the fog."

Cagney and Aidan reappeared. "We're ready."

Lucila clapped Cagney on the back. "Good! Because I have something wonderful I want to show you."

8

Gold

The cousins piled into the jeep and braced themselves. Lucila took off along the road at warp speed. She sped through crowded back streets, all the while pointing out interesting landmarks. For Cagney she pointed out clothing stores, for Aidan, the library and, for Tess, several bakeries. Honking and waving at passersby she squealed to a stop next to a large building.

"Gold!" said Aidan, reading the dazzling sign.

"What?" said Cagney.

"This is the Gold Museum." Lucila clambered out from behind the steering wheel. "Inca gold."

"Aren't the Inca the people who lived at Machu Picchu?" asked Lissy.

"Yes," said Lucila. "Come see."

The cousins bounded up the steps and into the lobby. Lucila pushed several crumpled notes into the ticket seller's hands, before wandering into the first of four large rooms. Each room was filled with gold, silver, ceramics and beautiful jewelry.

Lucila beckoned the cousins towards her and lowered her voice. "There is a legend: when the Spanish arrived in Peru, Atahualpa, the Inca King came to welcome them. But the Spanish were not there to be welcomed and before the king knew it, he had been captured."

"Oh! Poor Ata ... I mean Hupa ... I mean." Tess stopped and scratched her head. "Poor king."

"It gets worse," said Lucila. "Atahualpa decided to ask for his freedom and in return he promised to fill a room *full* of gold."

"I remember this." Lissy grinned. "Was the Spaniard called Pizarro?"

Lucila slapped Lissy on the shoulder. "Yes, you are the very smart girl."

Lissy checked to make sure her shoulder was still in one piece. "Thank you."

"Francisco Pizarro was a greedy man and he agreed to these terms. So the Inca King sent messages throughout his Empire to bring his ransom and the treasure poured into the city," explained Lucila.

"So they let him go?" asked Aidan.

"No! Instead of setting him free, they took him to the town square and he was killed." Lucila put her hands around her neck, stuck out her tongue and made a horrible strangling noise.

Tess winced. "Ooh! That's not very friendly."

Lucila frowned. "Yes leetle Puddleton. Pizarro was not the friendliest of men."

Cagney gingerly rubbed her neck. "You don't say."

Lucila held up a heavily ringed finger and beckoned the cousins closer. "But, what the Spanish did not know, was an even *greater* ransom was coming. Gold carried by 60,000 men from Ecuador with 12,000 armed guards was on its way."

"Whoa!" said Olivia. "That's a *lot* of gold."

"Yes! Yes!" said Lucila, warming to her topic. "The gold came from every temple and palace in

Quito. But! When the general of this army heard Atahualpa had been killed, he took the treasure and hid it." Lucila glanced around the room conspiratorially. "Even when he was captured, the general *never* told where the treasure was hidden."

"So what happened to it?" asked Aidan.

Lucila shrugged. "Nothing happened to it. Five hundred years later the gold has still not been found."

"Is that true?" asked Olivia.

Lucila traced an X across her chest. "It is true. The lost gold of the Inca is every treasure hunter's dream."

"So roughly speaking, how much is it worth?" asked Cagney. "Nine, ten million?"

"Almost. The last I read its current estimate is more like eight." Lucila's face broke into a large smile. "Billion."

Cagney's jaw dropped and, with much delight, Lucila lent forward and gently closed it.

The cousins continued wandering through the museum. Gold glinted from every direction; it was outrageous to think of a whole room crammed full of it.

"Look Olivia." Tess pointed at a glass cabinet filled with statues. "It's Cuddles."

Olivia peered over Tess' shoulder. Perched under a spotlight was a golden llama statue the size of her hand. With long straight ears and an even longer, straighter neck, there was no doubt about it, it was a gleaming, golden Cuddles.

Lucila bustled up behind them. "The Inca called themselves the Children of the Sun. The gold represents the sweat of the sun." She pointed to a smaller version of Cuddles in silver. "The silver, the tears of the moon."

Cagney wandered over to the cabinet and peered inside. Not much ever shocked Cagney but even she was still reeling from the thought of eight billion dollars' worth of gold hidden somewhere in the jungle. "So, how much is something like that?" she asked, pointing at the golden llama.

"It is priceless," said Lucila. "It is five hundred years old and made of solid gold. All of this is priceless."

"Aren't they scared someone will steal it?" asked Aidan.

"No, they cannot steal," said Lucila. "Look at the doors."

Aidan gave the doors a closer inspection. "They look like bank doors."

Lucila flung out her arms. "Yes, leettle Puddleton. The whole museum is one huge bank vault."

The five cousins wandered down the glittering corridor and entered the gift shop. Tess scooped up a beaded bracelet and dangled it across her wrist. "Wow, 144 dollars. That's a lot of money."

Aidan peaked over Tess' shoulder. "No, not dollars. The Peruvian currency is Nuevo Soles."

"Does that make it more dollars or less dollars?" asked Tess.

Aidan did the math in his head. "About 50 bucks."

Tess quickly replaced the brightly colored bracelet. "That's a lot of donuts."

Lucila swept into the gift shop and with her silver bangles jangling, beckoned the cousins towards her. "Come, leettle Puddletons. Next we visit the catacombs."

Tess looked puzzled. "What are catacombs?"

"It's where dead people are buried," replied Lissy.

Cagney froze. "She's joking, right?"

"It's just a couple of dead people." Olivia grinned. "How bad can it be?"

*
*   *
   *

9

The Dead

An hour later the cousins emerged from the Convent of San Francisco. Cagney's face resembled a frog's in both color and demeanor. Her eyes bulged, her cheeks puffed and if she could have said anything she would have croaked. Clutching a tissue to her nose Cagney gasped in the cool crisp air and sank onto the nearest bench.

Lissy collapsed beside her and shivered. "I thought you said it was just a couple of dead people?"

Olivia looked at her cousin puzzled. "There *were* a couple of dead people."

"Olivia! There were 80,000 skulls down there," squeaked Lissy.

Aidan batted his cousin on the back. "Olivia you are the official Queen of Understatement."

Olivia shrugged. "So I rounded down. Math has never been my strong point."

Lucila came puffing up behind them. "You like?"

Cagney rose unsteadily to her feet. "Actually, I think there are only so many dead people I can take in one sitting."

Lucila clapped Cagney on the back. "So, let's go eat."

Tess grinned. "Now you're talking."

The cousins followed Lucila through streets bustling with people.

"This is the Plaza Mayor," Lucila explained. "It is the heart of Lima."

The Plaza had a delicate fountain in the middle and several ornate buildings, sporting red and white flags, around the edges. Hurrying through, the cousins passed an imposing statue.

"Who's the guy in the weird looking clothes?" asked Olivia.

"Puh!" Lucila scowled. "That is Francisco Pizarro; he's the one who captured the Inca King. We no like him."

Tess cocked her head to one side and studied the statue. "Then why's there a statue of him on a horse?"

"Ssssh!" said Aidan. "He's the Spanish guy that invaded Peru."

"Spider said Pizarro founded Peru in 1532," said Lissy.

Tess was puzzled. "Wasn't there anyone living here before?"

"Yes," whispered Aidan. He moved Tess along. "That's the problem."

For a short, plump woman Lucila certainly could move, and the cousins sprinted after her. Cagney winced. The shoes that seemed so fabulous at the mall were annoying her. They were a teeny tiny bit too big and had the annoying habit of falling off. She squatted and adjusted the strap. She should have listened to Lissy and worn sneakers, but would rather eat grass than admit it. Besides, sneakers didn't go with her jeans. Lissy might not care what she looked like, but Lissy wasn't almost a teenager. Cagney was about to stand and hobble after them, when out of the corner of her eye she spotted something.

"Hey you!"

Cagney almost jumped out of her skin.

The voice came loud and clear across the plaza. "What are you doing?"

Cagney took a deep breath and ignored the people who were starting to stare.

"Come on, you're going to lose us if you don't keep up," continued Olivia.

Cagney crouched lower and performed a pitiful impression of a waddling duck. She flapped her hand in the air, waving Olivia towards her. "Get down."

Olivia sighed and strode back across the plaza. "Why are you crouching behind Pizarro's horse?"

"Look! Over there." Cagney jerked her head towards a man selling balloons.

Olivia's heel started to bounce, a sure sign she was irritated. "Aren't you a little old for balloons?"

Cagney snorted. Her shoes were currently eating her heels; she was in no mood for sarcasm. "Not the balloons. Look at the guy standing behind him."

Olivia glanced at a large black man in a large black suit.

Cagney raised her camera and snapped. "Does he remind you of anyone?"

Olivia smiled. "He sure does."

The cousins exited the Plaza Mayor and continued down a busy pedestrian street. Lima was such a fun, colorful city, thought Lissy, so full of energy and life.

Finally Lucila slowed her pace. She turned to the cousins and beamed. "We eat here. It is very good." Lucila plopped herself onto a chair outside a busy restaurant and handed each of the cousins a menu. The menu was extensive and the cousins were beyond hungry. As Tess explained, dead bodies will do that to you. Ten minutes later the food arrived and everyone dug in.

"Tess, you're not eating?" Lissy leaned forward and felt Tess' forehead. "Are you sick?"

Tess peered at the yellow substance covering her plate and gave it a poke. Tess had never met a chocolate bar she hadn't loved, but even by Tess' standards this was the weirdest chocolate she'd ever seen. "Where's the chocolate?"

Lucila laughed. "You ordered Choclo. Choclo is toasted corn on the cob with cheese and the chili sauce. It is a famous Peruvian dish."

"It's delicious," said Aidan, shoveling a spoonful of chili into his mouth.

Tess shrugged. She scooped up a huge mouthful and raised it to her lips. "I knew it was too good to be true."

Within minutes their plates were clean and their chairs pushed back. The cousins lounged contentedly, their legs rested, their bellies warm, and watched the citizens of Lima trickle by. A group of men in brightly colored ponchos gathered by the side of the road. They began playing a lilting melody and a crowd started to collect around them.

"Ooh, pretty." Tess tapped her feet and fingers in time with the music.

Cagney snapped a picture. Placing her camera on the table she wrinkled her nose. "What are those weird looking instruments?"

"Panpipes." Lucila smiled at Tess' enjoyment. "They are traditional Peruvian wind instruments."

Suddenly, a young man broke from the crowd. He wore jeans, a jacket and a puzzled look on his face. His hair had a military cut, and bulging from beneath the sleeves of his tight black tee were several well-developed muscles. Rapidly he swooped towards them, bent down and grasped Lucila around the waist. Lucila's knife clattered to the cobblestones and she gasped before looking up.

"Emilio!" Lucila grabbed the young man by the hair and gave it a playful tussle. Her face relaxed into a wide grin. "This is my son," she explained. "I did not know you were in Lima."

He bent and kissed his mother on both cheeks. "'Til tomorrow."

"Emilio, theez are my friends, the Puddletons."

Emilio caught his mother's eye and momentarily raised his eyebrow. Instantly the look was gone and he bowed gracefully. He scooted onto the chair beside his mother and placed her hand in his.

"Emilio is a very successful pilot. He flies the tourists to Machu Picchu."

"That was the picture we saw on Spider," said Lissy.

Olivia's eyes opened wide. "That must be the coolest job in the world."

"Yes. It is very cool." Emilio winked at his mother. "If you wish, I can take you. Every day I go deliver tourists and tomorrow I have an empty plane."

"Really?" Olivia glanced at the others. "Let's do it."

Cagney glared at her cousins and shook her head. "We can't."

"What do you mean we can't?" asked Olivia.

Cagney crossed her arms over her chest. "Because I don't know if you numbskulls remember, but we're *missing* a grandma."

Olivia let out an enormous sigh. "It's not my fault grandma went and got herself lost."

"No, Cagney's right," agreed Lissy. "I'm sorry, sir, but we really need to stay here until Grandma Callie gets, erm, un-lost."

Olivia folded her arms and harrumphed.

Emilio shrugged and ruffled the top of Olivia's short, black hair. "Consider it an open invitation. You would be my guests." He slapped a hand over his heart and grinned. "It would be my honor."

*
* *
*

10

The Dark Shadow

The cousins waved goodbye to Lucila as she zoomed around the corner in a puff of fumes. Tired after a long day, the five shuffled into the lobby. Señor Gustavo was chatting to Gabriela and, if Cagney wasn't mistaken, he was sucking in his stomach.

"Ah, here are my Puddelitos. Señor Gustavo has a message for you." Señor Gustavo leaned over the desk and handed a note to Cagney.

Cagney peered at the familiar handwriting. "It's from Grandma."

"Grandma's here?" Lissy's eyes darted around the foyer.

"I am sorry Puddelitos, but you just missed her."

"What?" Cagney looked outraged. "She's gone again?"

Señor Gustavo waved his hands nonchalantly in the air. "Puddelitos, you cannot expect a woman like your grandmother to hang around and wait."

Lissy frowned. "We can't?"

"No, we can't," replied Señor Gustavo.

"Why was she here then?" asked Aidan.

"Tea." Señor Gustavo sighed. "We had a nice cup of tea and a plate of sticky buns. Ah!" he said with a toothy grin. "It was just like old times."

"Señorita Puddleton was at the hotel?" asked Gabriela.

"Yes, yes. It was wonderful to see her again. She is so funny, she makes Señor Gustavo's belly shake with laughter."

Cagney raised an eyebrow. "Grandma's funny?"

"Of course." Señor Gustavo beamed. "She is a wonderful mimic."

"Are you sure we're talking about the same grandma?" asked Olivia. "You know, short, grey hair, yells if you eat too many cookies."

Señor Gustavo sighed. "The one and the same."

"Did *you* see her?" Lissy turned to Gabriela.

"Unfortunately not. I arrived only a few minutes before you."

Lissy frowned. "I wish we hadn't missed her. I wanted to tell her about the gold museum."

"I am disappointed too," said Gabriela. "Your grandma sounds fascinating."

"Believe me," said Olivia, "she gets more fascinating by the second."

"Come on Cagney. Don't just stand there." Aidan plopped his chin onto Cagney's shoulder. "Read the note."

Cagney tore open the envelope and read.

> *My friends tell me you are having a lot of fun.*
> *I hear they are taking good care of you.*
> *Enjoy Lima and keep out of mischief.*
> *Stay at the hotel and I will see you soon.*
> *Grandma"*

"Do you think she's okay?" asked Lissy.

"She had tea and sticky buns," said Tess. "Sounds like she's okay to me."

Gabriela ushered the cousins towards the courtyard. "Come. Tell me what you did today."

Aidan hurried to open the door. "Lucila showed us all kinds of cool things."

"Skulls," said Olivia.

"Gold," said Cagney.

"Chocolate," said Tess, "well, kind of."

"Yes, yes. That sounds wonderful." Distracted, Gabriela glanced around the courtyard. "Look, Cook is playing Sapo with her grandson, Santiago. I am sure you will not have played it before. You should join her. It will help take your mind off your grandma."

With her white apron, white hat and ruddy pink cheeks Lissy thought Cook looked exactly like Mrs. White in *Clue*. Gabriela turned to leave.

"Aren't you coming?" asked Aidan.

Gabriela pinched Aidan's cheek. Scarlet crept from his collar to his curls. "I have some things I need to take care of. I will see you later, no?"

The five wandered into the courtyard. In the far corner Cook was helping her grandson aim a small coin at a wooden chest.

"You guys go ahead." Cagney turned back towards the hotel. "I'm going to run to the room and change my battery."

Cagney headed through the lobby and up the stairs. At the top she fumbled in her bag for the key. A loud click made her look up. Down the far end of the hallway was a shadowy figure.

Cagney pushed her glasses along her nose and peered into the gloom. "Er, hello?"

The shadow didn't reply, but edged further along the corridor, opened a door and slipped behind it.

"Cagney, come look at the Sapo game." Lissy sat with Santiago curled upon her lap. She had a way with younger children; she was, as Olivia would say with a snort, a child magnet.

Lissy pointed at a square wooden box. On the top crouched a metal toad with its mouth open. Surrounding it were several little holes. A series of different numbers lined the front of the box.

"You have to get coins in the holes and then you count your score by the numbers on the front," explained Lissy. "If you get the coin in the toad you get the most points."

"Santiago's got the coin in the toad's mouth three times," said Aidan.

Tess scooped up a bunch of coins that lay scattered on the courtyard tiles. "I've not even hit the box yet."

Cagney had no intention of playing some silly frog game. A more pressing matter needed her attention. With a series of subtle head jerks and widening eye movements Cagney eventually caught Olivia's attention.

Olivia moved towards her. "You know you've got a serious twitch, right?"

Cagney ran her fingers through her hair. "It's not a twitch. I've got– "

"Lice?" Aidan backed away. "You don't have that again, do you?"

Cagney bit her tongue and tried not to hyperventilate.

"I hate it when that happens." Tess turned to Cook and pointed towards her cousin. "Cagney's got– "

But Tess' explanation of what her cousin may or may not have was silenced, as Cagney took her by the arm and hauled her towards an empty table. One by one the cousins plopped into chairs.

"Okay, lice girl, what's up?" asked Olivia, grinning.

Cagney composed herself and, swiveling her head like a periscope, scanned the courtyard to make sure she could not be overheard. She lowered her voice. "Guys, something really strange just happened. When I reached the top of the stairs I heard someone opening and closing a door."

Olivia leaned back and sighed. "I'm surprised you haven't called the cops already."

Cagney batted Olivia in exasperation.

"Well! This *is* a hotel," said Olivia. "What do you expect? You think guests should get in through the window?"

"Obviously not," said Cagney. "But, Miss Clever Clogs, they were coming out of our room."

"What?" Olivia jumped to her feet. "Why didn't you say so?"

Cagney motioned for Olivia to sit and warily eyed the courtyard. "I'm sure I saw someone slip out of our room and when I shouted hello, they disappeared."

"It's pretty dark in that hallway," said Aidan. "Are you sure your imagination wasn't getting the better of you?"

Cagney scowled. She pushed her glasses far up the bridge of her nose. "Do I look like my imagination is getting the better of me?"

"She has a point," said Tess.

"Could you tell who it was?" asked Lissy.

Cagney checked over her shoulder and leaned forward. "That's the really strange thing; I think it was Gabriela."

11

Stranger in the Night

"Talking of strange," said Olivia. "Cagney and I saw someone we know in the Plaza today."

"But we don't *know* anyone here," said Lissy.

"The person we saw wasn't from here." Cagney flicked through her pictures.

Olivia nodded. "They were from Texas."

"Mrs. Snoops is in Lima?" Tess asked, incredulously.

Cagney raised her eyes. "Not Mrs. Snoops. Sneezy."

"Who?" asked Tess.

"You know." Olivia made a snuffling noise and let out a gigantic sneeze.

"The pet sitter?" asked Tess.

Cagney stopped flicking and turned her camera around. On her viewfinder was a tiny picture of a man dressed all in black. She zoomed in for the others to see.

Tess peered intently at the picture. "Is he meant to have a balloon in front of his face?"

Cagney flipped the camera around, peered at the viewfinder and scowled.

"Aha!" Aidan pointed a finger towards Cagney. "I told you he was at the airport. But would anyone listen to me? No they wouldn't."

"Ah, put a cork in it. We believe you now, don't we?"

"But who's looking after Chaos and Hiss?" asked Tess.

"I think the bigger question is what Grandma's pet sitter is doing in Lima," said Lissy.

"Can't tell you that," said Aidan. "But it sure seems weird."

After a short nap the cousins were back in the courtyard. Exhausted from their long day, they sat slumped around the table relaxing after a luxurious meal. Lissy had figured out there was a reason Cook was so plump – the food was incredible.

Cagney browsed through the photos she had taken that day. Aidan read his library book, *Dragons I Have Known and Loved.* Tess and Olivia played blackjack, and Lissy surfed the web.

"Did you know they had penguins in Peru?" Lissy said, tapping away at Spider.

"Really? Isn't it too hot for them?" asked Aidan.

"Apparently not. Peru is also home to chinchillas, tapirs, giant armadillos and twenty percent of the world's butterflies. There's also a lake called Titicaca."

Olivia smirked. "Yeah right."

"No, really," said Lissy. "It's the highest lake in the world you can sail on. If you went from one side to the other you'd be in Bolivia."

"I still don't believe it," said Olivia. "The name Titicaca is just too weird."

"Tess, get this," said Lissy. "They found a hot pink dolphin in the Amazon."

"It's really pink?" asked Tess.

Cagney placed her camera on the table and leaned back. "I can guarantee it's not going to be blue."

"Wow, can we go see it?" asked Tess.

"Nope, the Amazon is way northeast of us. Besides you'd never find it. Spider says the Amazon is over a mile wide in places."

The cousins fell into silence. Learning things about Peru took their minds off the nasty thought that Gabriela had been spying on them.

Aidan closed his library book and glanced around the deserted courtyard. "I wonder where Gabriela and Pietro are."

"D'ya think we should ask her what she was doing in our room?" asked Olivia, her eyes sparkling.

Lissy shook her head. She didn't like confrontation and accusing Gabriela of breaking into their room would almost guarantee confrontation. "I don't think so."

Olivia scowled as Tess plunked 'twenty one' onto the table. "I guess you're right. Cagney wasn't even sure it was her. Her glasses probably got misted up. They're definitely not as good ever since she broke them. Look at them, they're all wonky."

Cagney tried to kick Olivia under the table, but missed and instead got Aidan smartly on the shin.

Lissy sighed in relief. Even though she and Olivia were polar opposites, Lissy couldn't help but admire her cousin. Olivia didn't care what people thought of her. She was brave and said what was on her mind; unfortunately what was on her mind often got her, and those all around her, into trouble. Lissy could spend an entire lifetime without trouble and it still wouldn't be enough.

Tess stifled a yawn. "I like her. My fluffy pink slippers have a good feeling about her. Let's not make her feel bad."

"Come on sleepy head," said Aidan, rubbing his leg. "Let's get you to bed."

Lissy closed Spider. "Me too, I'm beat."

The cousins packed up their things. They traipsed through the lobby and up the old rickety staircase. The dark hallway loomed in front of them. Aidan tapped Cagney on the shoulder.

"Boo," he said softly.

Cagney jumped a mile and swiped at her brother. "Not funny."

"Is too," said Aidan, rubbing his shoulder.

"Oh, come on, there's nothing to be afraid of." Olivia marched down the hallway, jammed the key in the lock and plunged through the doorway. She threw her things at the bottom of her bed and crawled under the red woven blankets. Within minutes everyone was fast asleep. It was just what someone, lurking along the corridor, was waiting for.

Cagney was dreaming. She dreamed someone was looking in the wardrobe. She dreamed someone was looking behind the curtains. However, she wasn't dreaming when that person stubbed their toe on the bottom of her bed.

"Drat!" said a voice.

Cagney sprang up just in time to see the door to the hallway slowly close. She shook Lissy who was sleeping peacefully beside her. Cagney fumbled for her glasses. "Lissy, did you hear that?"

"*Mmmmm.* The square root of 9,604 is..." Lissy mumbled.

Good Lord, thought Cagney. *The girl even dreams in problems.* Cagney shoved her glasses onto her nose and squinted around the pitch-black room. "Guys, I think someone was in here."

Aidan bolted upright. "Who was it ... what did you ... where is he?"

Tess let out a humongous snore from the bed opposite.

Olivia pushed herself into a sitting position and rubbed her eyes. "Somebody get the light."

Aidan stumbled to the door and flipped the switch. He looked around the room. Cagney and Olivia were wide-awake, Lissy lay comatose and Tess was sprawled on top of the blankets, her bottom poking into the air like half a McDonald's arch.

Olivia rolled over and came face to feet with Tess' toes. Olivia sighed; sleeping with Tess was like sleeping with a squirming bag of puppies. She grabbed a foot and pulled.

Tess wiggled her toes and stretched. "Good morning," she yawned.

Olivia shook her sister. "Wake-up, sleepy-head. Cagney thinks someone was in our room."

Lissy pulled a pillow over her head and rolled over. "Not again."

"Really?" said Tess, rising. "I don't think my pink flannel pj's can cope with such excitement."

The cousins crawled from beneath their blankets and piled onto Cagney and Lissy's bed.

Cagney pulled the blankets tight around her neck. "Honestly guys, I'm not making it up."

Lissy emerged from under the pillow and pushed a curl from her eyes. "The thing is not to panic!"

"I'm NOT panicking!" yelled Cagney.

Lissy pounded her ear with the palm of her hand. "Don't worry Cagney; I never liked the hearing in that ear much anyway."

Cagney scowled.

"Tell us exactly what you saw," said Aidan.

"I didn't see anything," Cagney moaned. "But I felt someone bump the bed. I heard them cry out as they stubbed their toe on the bedpost, but by the time I'd grabbed my glasses they'd gone."

"Wow, that's got to hurt," said Tess. "I hate it when I stub my toe."

"Serves them right for snooping in our room," said Olivia.

"So you do believe me?" Cagney let out a sigh.

"I believe you, sis. I left my library book on top of the chest of drawers and now it's on the chair."

"Spider was by the side of my bed," said Lissy, "and now she's pushed under."

Olivia jumped off the bed, scooped down and ran a finger along the leg of the four-poster. She grimaced. Rising, she held out a finger covered with a smear of blood.

Aidan felt his throat go cold and turned his head.

Olivia snatched up a Kleenex and wiped the blood off her index finger. "Yep, we've had company alright."

"We'd better go through everything and make sure nothing's been stolen," suggested Lissy.

"We should probably lock the door as well, right?" said Tess.

"Excellent idea. Aidan, lock the door," Cagney commanded.

Aidan saluted his sister and headed for the door. He dragged the heavy oak chair in front of it and turned the lock.

"Good thinking, batman," said Olivia. "Now if someone breaks in, at least they'll have a place to sit."

As soon as the lock clicked, the cousins scooted to the end of their beds and rifled through their bags.

"Oh no!" cried Tess.

"What is it? What's missing?" Cagney bounded across the room.

Tess spun around. "My donut's gone."

Cagney stopped in mid bound. She rolled her eyes. "You ate that earlier, you big lummox."

"And I have the crumbs in my bed to prove it," said Olivia.

"Oh, yeah," said Tess. "Sorry."

"What on earth are they looking for?" asked Cagney.

"I don't know. Everything of value is still here," said Aidan.

"Passports, money, camera and Spider are all accounted for," said Lissy.

Olivia swept several stray donut crumbs from the covers before clambering back into bed. "I don't know what they're looking for, but they're sure going to have a sore toe tomorrow."

12

The Hidden Chamber

The cousins arrived at breakfast bleary-eyed and confused. None of them slept well after the intruder and in desperation they had taken turns keeping watch.

"Look, there's Gabriela and Pietro," said Lissy, as they traipsed across the courtyard.

Aidan adjusted his already immaculate collar, pulled back his shoulders and sucked in his miniscule tummy.

Cagney tapped him on the shoulder. "Act normal."

Aidan squinted over his shoulder at his sister. "I am acting normal. I am the definition of normal. When you look up "normal" in the dictionary, there's a picture of me ... looking normal." He turned in time to see a small wicker chair pushed back from its table.

To be fair, Aidan tried his best to avoid it, but it was too late. His knees hit the seat. His body lurched forward. His hands hit the back of the chair and the entire thing flipped – including Aidan.

Cagney gave him the Look of Death as Lissy yanked him to his feet.

"Nice!" Olivia grinned as she sidestepped her cousin. "Real classy."

"You'd make a great circus clown, Aidan," said Tess, as she skipped on by.

Aidan adjusted his polo shirt and made a mental note to talk to his cousins about their serious lack of empathy.

Gabriela looked up and waved enthusiastically.

"Hi," shouted Tess.

Cagney caught hold of her cousin's pigtail and pulled her steadily towards the nearest table. "Are you nuts?"

Tess pushed Cagney away and straightened the large pink bows in her hair. "What did I do?"

"You're only waving to the person we think broke into our room last night," said Cagney.

"Oh, that." Tess plopped onto a chair and stuffed the edge of a large napkin down the neck of her sweater. "Don't worry I'm sure it wasn't her."

"Really?" asked Lissy. "What makes you so sure?"

"She's too nice," said Tess. "Plus, my pink fuzzy sweater's telling me not to worry about her."

Cagney rolled her eyes. "She's crazy."

"Oh, don't say that," said Tess. "I think she's sweet."

"Not Gabriela." Cagney pulled out a chair and sank into it. "You."

The cousins sat a couple of tables away from Gabriela and Pietro and ordered hot chocolate and tamales. Within seconds the cousins were inhaling five steaming bowls of chocolatey goodness. Tess sighed contentedly.

Olivia unraveled her silverware and flapped out the creases in her napkin. In mid flap she let the cloth float gently to the floor. Winking at Aidan, Olivia bent under the table to retrieve it. Seconds later she reappeared.

She combed a hand through her un-brushed hair and scowled. "Rats! Gabriela has loafers on. I can't see if her toe is bruised."

"Figures," said Cagney. "Can anyone hear what they're saying?"

"Nope. But it doesn't matter, they're speaking Spanish," said Lissy.

Aidan cocked his head to the side and frowned. "Something about digging."

Olivia stared at him. "That *Spanish for the Seriously Stupid* book is really working."

Aidan grinned. "It really is."

The cousins ate breakfast quietly, trying to let Aidan hear what Gabriela and Pietro were discussing. But the two of them had their heads close together and Aidan found it impossible. After a few minutes Gabriela and Pietro pushed back their chairs and headed across the courtyard.

"*Buenos Dias*," Gabriela said, smiling. Pietro nodded curtly.

"Hi," said Tess.

The cousins watched the couple disappear through the French doors into the lobby.

Olivia's eyes twinkled. "Did anybody notice anything strange about Pietro?"

"You mean apart from the fact that he wasn't scowling?" said Cagney.

"Yeah," said Tess. "The poor thing was limping; he must have hurt his foot."

There was silence.

"She'll get it eventually," said Olivia.

Tess looked around. "Get what?"

Olivia hummed the theme from Jeopardy.

"Ooh!" said Tess. "You mean the man, the toe, the ... ooh!"

"Told you she'd get it," said Olivia.

Lissy sighed. It was bad enough thinking of Gabriela breaking into their room. The thought of Pietro searching through their things made her faint. "We shouldn't jump to conclusions. We don't know that for sure."

"It sure looks like it," said Olivia.

"But what in Great Aunt Maud's name are they looking for?" asked Aidan.

"Maybe they weren't looking for anything." Cagney pursed her lips in concentration. "Maybe they were leaving something."

"But why would anyone do that?" asked Lissy.

"I don't know," said Cagney, "but if nothing's missing, maybe something was left. We need to go search the room right now."

Aidan shrugged. "It's a mystery to me, but I guess it's worth a try."

"Ooh!" said Tess. "I love mysteries."

Olivia's dimple broke onto her cheek as she grinned widely. "Then let's go solve one."

The cousins scraped back their chairs, dashed upstairs and along the hallway. The room was a jumbled mess of clothes, shoes, bags and souvenirs.

Cagney held up a hand. "First let's tidy. We'll never find anything in this mess."

Aidan surveyed his pile of clothes folded neatly on the floor. "You're joking, right?"

"You make your bed, and now you have to tidy it." Cagney once again misquoted.

Aidan grabbed a handful of his clothes and placed them on the end of his bed. "And I'm done!"

Cagney gave him a look and he reluctantly picked up a few more. The mess turned out to be mostly Tess', and ten minutes later, with significant help from Lissy, the room was as tidy as it was ever going to be. Cagney surveyed the room and nodded approval. "Right. Let's do this. I'll search the balcony."

"I'll take the armoire," said Lissy.

"Bathroom for me," said Aidan.

Tess plucked up a stray donut crumb and popped it into her mouth. "Remind me what we're looking for again?"

"I don't know," said Cagney. "But I have a feeling we'll know it if we find it."

Aidan reappeared from the bathroom. He leapt onto the bed and grabbed his library book. "This is ridiculous. We're never going to find anything."

Tess plopped down beside him. "Yep, I've looked everywhere. Well, everywhere four feet and under."

"It's hopeless; we don't even know what we're hunting for," said Olivia.

The cousins collapsed on their beds and stared at the canopies above them.

Cagney frowned. "I was sure we were on the right track."

"Me too." Lissy brushed a cobweb from her curls. "But, we've searched everywhere. I even examined the back of the armoire, in case there was a secret compartment."

"Wait!" Olivia sat upright. "There's one place we haven't looked."

"Where?" asked Lissy.

"Up," said Olivia.

"Up what?" asked Tess.

Olivia pointed at the ceiling. "Up there! Aidan, let me stand on your shoulders."

Aidan wedged the book under his pillow and slid from the bed. Olivia kicked off her sneakers, jumped onto his back and clambered onto his shoulders. Her arms outstretched like a scarecrow she quickly got her balance.

"Now walk slowly around the room."

Aidan wrinkled his nose and sniffed. "Have you washed your feet today?"

Olivia grunted.

Aidan took a stifled gasp and covered his nose with his hand. "Forget today, how about in the last week?"

Aidan took great pride in his appearance. His shirts were always pressed, his shoes always shined. Aidan loved his cousin, but cleanliness was not one of Olivia's highest priorities.

Olivia bent down and swatted the top of his head. "Just walk, will you."

Aidan scowled. "I'm walking, I'm walking."

Aidan paced slowly while Olivia pushed the top of the walls and prodded the ceiling. The two cousins moved around the room until Olivia let out a yell. "I've found something!"

"What is it?" asked Lissy.

"It's a hidden chamber. Here, above Aidan's bed."

"Is there gold in it?" asked Aidan.

"Jewelry?" said Cagney.

"A cheeseburger with fries?" suggested Tess.

Olivia dropped from Aidan's shoulders and opened her fist. The cousins stared. Inside her hand was a small piece of paper.

13

Breaking the Code

Olivia unfolded the paper and read. "877.018."

Cagney grabbed it and turned it over. There it was. Absolutely nothing. Cagney launched herself onto the bed. "Good grief. What a letdown."

"But what does it mean?" Lissy plucked the paper out of Cagney's fingers and held it to the light.

"I don't know," said Olivia, "but it's got to mean something. Why else would it be so well hidden?"

"Think," said Lissy. "We can figure this out. There's got to be a logical explanation."

"Maybe it's a bank account," said Olivia.

Lissy shook her head. "No. Bank accounts have more numbers."

"Ooh! Maybe we found the secret code to a vault crammed with millions of dollars," said Tess.

"Millions of Nuevo Soles," Lissy corrected.

"I'm not thinking about the currency," said Tess. "I'm thinking about the millions."

Aidan scratched his head. "Could it be map co-ordinates?"

Cagney gave her brother one of her best looks. "No one is to say *anything* until I'm certain you're right," she demanded.

The five were silent. It was a complete mystery. Each cousin assumed their best thinking position. Lissy perched on the edge of the chair, her elbows on her knees, her face in her hands. Olivia paced the room, a frown wrinkling her nose. Tess lay on her back, twirled her feet in the air and pulled back the first strand of a plump yellow banana.

"I know!" Lissy let out a small squeal and promptly fell off the chair. "It's a telephone number."

Cagney raised a bored eyebrow. "But it doesn't have the right number of digits for a telephone number."

"Hmm! Not for the States." Lissy turned her back on Cagney. "But for here it might."

Olivia snatched the phone and tossed it to Aidan. "Only one way to find out."

Aidan punched in the numbers. The five held their breath as they heard a voice answer on the other end. Aidan listened, frowned and replaced the receiver.

Cagney sat up. "Well? For goodness sake, tell us what they said."

Aidan shook his head. "They said, this number's disconnected."

"Great. Just great." Cagney lurched onto the bed and muttered something none too charitable.

Aidan slouched onto his bed, grabbed his library book and sank into the pillows.

"Have you still not finished that silly dragon book?" Cagney was now itching for a fight.

"It is *not* a silly dragon book," muttered Aidan. He opened the book wide and held it in front of his face. He knew his sister too well. If he didn't look at her maybe he could avoid a fight. He could almost have got away with it, if it hadn't been for one tiny, misplaced sentence that slipped from his lips. "And besides, it's better than your silly fashion magazines."

Lissy winced and shut her eyes. Cagney did not like to have her magazines referred to as silly. Aidan was about to get a tongue-lashing and everybody knew it. But the tongue-lashing never came. Tentatively, Lissy opened one eye and then the other. Cagney was staring at Aidan, a glazed look across her face.

Lissy reached out and touched Cagney's arm. "Cagney, are you okay?"

Slowly Cagney tore her eyes away. She looked Lissy full in the face. "I know what it is."

Aidan dropped the book.

Tess stuffed the remaining half of the banana into her mouth. "What?" she mumbled.

"Aidan's book," said Cagney. "Look at the cover."

Aidan flipped the book face down and the cousins gathered round.

"*Dragons I Have Known and Loved* by Esther Plunkett." Tess scratched her head. "It's a very silly name."

"Yes, but what's that got to do with the numbers?" asked Olivia.

Cagney rolled her eyes. A smug look crept across her face. "Are you guys blind? Look!"

The cousins peered at the book. They peered harder.

Cagney shook her head. "The spine, you nincompoops! The spine!"

Olivia bent forward. On the base of the spine was a small white tag with five numbers printed on it. "398.245."

"It's the same number format," said Lissy.

Aidan smacked his hand on his forehead. "The Dewey Decimal System. All library books have a code on them so they can be easily found."

"Exactly." Cagney shrugged on her coat and headed towards the door.

Tess tossed the banana peel in the general direction of the trash. "Ooh! Are we going out? Where are we going?"

"The library," said Cagney. "It's right around the corner. Lucila pointed it out yesterday."

Olivia looked unconvinced. "You really think that's what it is?"

"I'm positive." Cagney stopped. "Well not positive, but it's worth a try. Besides, we've got nothing else to do!"

The cousins threw on their coats and hurried along the hallway. At the top of the stairs they came to an abrupt halt. A raspy voice echoed through the lobby.

"Pietro," whispered Lissy.

"Ooh he's mad," said Tess.

"There's a surprise," said Olivia.

Aidan edged forward. "He's checking out, and so is Gabriela."

The cousins crouched in the shadows and peered between the banisters. Pietro was in the process of stabbing a finger dangerously close to Señor Gustavo's glistening nose.

Aidan shook his head. "He's such a bully."

With one last glare Pietro slung his backpack across his shoulders and herded Gabriela towards the exit.

"Oh no," whispered Cagney. "I never got to show her my pictures of Lima."

"Considering how many times she and Pietro have been in our room," said Olivia, "they've probably seen them all."

Cagney shrugged. "I hate it when you're right."

Pietro grasped the door and flung it open. With one final apologetic smile, Gabriela hurried through it.

"Poor Gabriela," said Lissy.

"She certainly doesn't look very happy," said Aidan.

Tess wrinkled her nose. "Nor would you if you had to hang out with Mr. Grumpy pants."

Lissy stifled a giggle.

"Come on slow pokes." Olivia leapt to her feet. "They should be gone by now."

Olivia flew down the stairs and through the lobby. She burst through the large wooden doors and bumped straight into the back of a tall, thin man. Olivia bounced off Pietro's backpack and landed bottom down on the sidewalk. Gabriela extended a hand and sprung Olivia to her feet.

"Oopsies!" Olivia brushed off her pants. "Er! Fancy seeing you here."

"Fancy!" said Pietro.

"We're going to the library," said Tess.

Tess clapped a hand over her mouth. Lissy coughed loudly and Cagney gave Tess one of her death ray stares. But it was too late. The cousins gaped at her in horror.

"To get a book," stammered Lissy.

"We like to read." Aidan shook his head, amazed at his ridiculousness. If there was an Olympic award for stupidity, surely he had just won it.

Pietro scowled at them. "How nice." His voice was pure ice and Aidan felt a chill run down to his toes.

Seconds later, a yellow taxi drew up in front of the hotel and the driver jumped out. Without another glance at the cousins, Pietro threw his backpack at the driver and yanked open the door.

He pushed Gabriela into the cab and, following her in, yelled, "Jorge Chavez."

Gabriela turned and gave the cousins a half-hearted smile. "Goodbye."

"See ya," said Olivia, already halfway down the street.

"Ah phooey!" said Tess "Do you think they're on to us?"

"Probably not." Aidan shook his head. "But I'm sure they think we're the biggest bunch of idiots they've ever met."

Tess shrugged. "Oh, well that's all right then."

The cousins tore along the narrow sidewalks of Lima. They flew past brightly painted facades, past open doorways and shops so small you couldn't swing a cat. Finally, in the distance, they saw the familiar sight of the library. They bounded up the steps and pushed open the ornate wooden doors.

Cagney took a deep breath. "Here goes nothing."

14

Treasure

The cousins entered the coolness of the library and slowly ascended several marble steps. The library was grand. The library was impressive. The library was as silent as a wilted cactus.

Aidan scratched his head. "Where should we look?"

"There's an information desk." Lissy pointed into the gloom. "We can ask there."

The cousins hurried across the lobby and slid to a halt in front of a large, semi-circular desk.

"Hello." Cagney held out the piece of paper and flapped it around. "We would like to know how to find a book with this number."

An elderly librarian gazed at the cousins. His once black hair was now streaked with white and his face looked like he had spent most of it under a cruel sun. If there was a competition for most prune-like features, he would have won hands down. The human prune shrugged his shoulders.

"He doesn't understand you," said Lissy.

Cagney rolled her eyes. "You don't say."

"*Hola,*" said Aidan. "*Nos podria ayudar a encontrar este numero?*"

Lissy's mouth gaped. She stared at Aidan in astonishment. "Impressive."

The librarian smiled a wrinkled smile and shook his head. "*No se admiten turistas,*" he said gently.

"What did he say?" asked Cagney.

"He said tourists aren't allowed in the library; it's only for residents."

"What makes him think we're not residents?" asked Cagney.

This time it was Aidan's turn to give his sister a look.

A sudden thud made the cousins spin around. Tess lay crumpled on the floor like a melted strawberry milkshake.

"Tess!" screamed Lissy.

Olivia turned white. "Oh no! If anything happens to Tess, mom's going to kill me."

The cousins leapt into action. Aidan scrunched down and felt for a pulse. Lissy fanned Tess' face and Olivia sunk to her knees, grabbed her sister's head and yanked it onto her lap.

"Don't panic." Cagney leaned against the desk. "She's only fainted."

"Should I slap her?" asked Olivia.

"Olivia!" Lissy was shocked. "You can't slap her."

"Why not?" said Olivia. "It works in the movies."

The librarian prized himself out of his seat. Once standing, he resembled the number seven. The prune sighed deeply and tottered towards the opening at the back of the desk.

"Pssst," Tess opened an eye. "Cagney, Aidan, quick, go now while no one's watching."

Lissy gasped.

"Tess Li Wei Puddleton – you rat fink. You scared the living daylights out of me." Olivia let her sister's head slide off her lap and thump onto the floor.

Tess squinted at her sister. "Hey, don't think I didn't hear that slap remark."

Lissy glanced around. The librarian was shuffling towards them. "Quick, go now."

Cagney and Aidan didn't need any further encouragement. Crouching low, they edged around the far side of the desk, raced to the back of the lobby and flew up the steps.

Aidan reached the top of the stairs and clutched his side. "Which way?" he said panting.

Cagney stared down the long corridor. "Oh, let me think about the last time I was here." She glared at Aidan. "How would I know?"

Aidan spied a map on the wall. He inched the piece of paper out of Cagney's fingers and studied the diagram. His finger traced the numbers. He pointed to the left. "This way."

The corridor led to an ancient looking door with a panel of glass at the top. Grasping the handle,

Aidan pried open the door and peered in. The room had old-fashioned wood paneling and the overpowering stuffy smell of used books. A narrow corridor divided two sections, but other than that, the space was ceiling high with books. Aidan followed Cagney into the room. It felt claustrophobic and he ran his fingers around the inside of his collar.

Aidan smiled at a passerby. "Try to blend in."

"Oh yeah." Cagney shook her head. "Two pale-faced kids with light hair. We'll fit right in."

Cagney and Aidan tiptoed along the narrow path. Their heads turned from side to side, like watching a tennis match, as they scanned the numbers on the shelves.

"Hey, sis, I think this is it." Aidan gazed at the scrap of paper. "877.018."

"I'll take this side and you take that," said Cagney, "and look between the books. I bet whatever it is has been pushed in-between."

Cagney and Aidan pulled out book after book, a pile growing steadily taller on the floor behind them.

"I've found something," said Aidan.

Cagney span around. "What is it?"

Aidan pulled out a piece of paper and read.

"*leche*

pan

queso"

Cagney frowned. "What does it mean?"

"It means someone lost their shopping list." He stuffed the note back between the shelves.

"Wait! I have something." Cagney reached under the shelf and pulled a face. "Ugh, forget it. It's only a piece of gum."

Aidan pulled out a small book on Latin humor. He opened it and gave it a good shake. Across the aisle Cagney saw something small and white drop into the palm of Aidan's hand.

"I've got it!"

"Put it in your pocket quick," whispered Cagney.

Aidan slipped the paper into his jacket pocket. "Why are we whispering?"

"Because ..." Cagney grimaced, "we have company."

Aidan glanced up as a shadow fell across his face. The end of the aisle was blocked by a very disgruntled looking security guard. Aidan took a step back and plastered a nonchalant grin on his face. *What had Lucila said about people from Lima? They were friendly, right?* Aidan had the distinct impression the security guard was from out of town. Way out.

Aidan gulped. "*Hola?*"

The security guard did *not* smile back. Seconds later, Cagney and Aidan were being hauled by the scruff of their necks through the library. The heavy wooden doors were yanked open and their behinds pushed into the foggy Lima day. Lissy, Tess and Olivia sat on the steps waiting for them.

Olivia jumped to her feet. "Did you find anything?"

Aidan straightened his collar. "Sure did."

The cousins gathered around. Aidan fished in his pocket and brought out a small white object.

Lissy frowned. "It's another piece of paper."

"But there's something hard inside." Carefully, Aidan unfolded the paper.

Cagney looked at the small square piece of plastic in Aidan's hand. A smile of recognition grew across her face. "It's a camera flash card."

Cagney snatched the flash card from Aidan's hand and took off running down the road.

"Where are you going?" asked Olivia, hurrying to keep up.

"Where do you think I'm going?" Cagney shouted over her shoulder. "I'm going to the hotel to download the flash card."

Up in the room Aidan closed the curtains. Lissy plugged in Spider and Cagney inserted the flash card. One by one, pictures flashed onto the screen.

"Let me take a look at that piece of paper," said Olivia, while they were waiting for the pictures to finish downloading.

In their haste, no one had looked at the paper that contained the flash card.

Olivia frowned. "There's something written on it, but I think it's in Spanish."

Aidan stared at the paper. "Yeah, that's Spanish, but I can translate it with my *Spanish for the Seriously Stupid* book."

Lissy gasped. "Guys, I think you'd better come take a look."

Tess bounded across the room. "Ooh! What are the pictures of?"

Lissy's eyes widened. She spun Spider around for the others to see. "Treasure!"

15

Disaster

The cousins gathered around Spider and gaped in disbelief. Sparkling gold necklaces, bracelets and masks filled the screen.

Tess jabbed her finger towards Spider. "Ooh! That golden llama looks twice as big as the one we saw in the museum."

"Lucila said that one was priceless," said Lissy.

Tess tilted her head to the side and wrinkled her nose. "If that one was priceless, this one must be super priceless."

Lissy flicked through the images. Picture after picture showed piles of shimmering gold and dazzling jewels.

"So what are they?" asked Cagney. "Do you think they were taken at the Gold Museum?"

"I don't think so." Lissy paused at a close-up detailing an ornately studded crown. "This gold is lying on the ground like it's in the jungle. Like it's lost."

"Wow!" Tess clamped a hand over her mouth. "The lost gold of the Inca."

Aidan closed his *Spanish for the Seriously Stupid* book and grinned. "Got it."

"Well?" Cagney marched towards her brother. "Don't stand there looking all smug, tell us what it says."

Aidan cleared his throat. "Well, don't quote me. But it's something like this.

> *I cannot wait any longer*
> *He is starting to suspect*
> *I have left the pictures*
> *I have to go back to the dig*
> *Please get them to the right people*
> *I am depending on you*
> *G"*

"Ooh! It's a poem." Tess bounced onto the bed. "I like poems."

Aidan scratched his head. "Not so much a poem as a riddle."

"Riddle, schmiddle," said Cagney. "Just tell us what it means, Einstein."

Aidan shrugged. "Sorry, sis, I'm only the translator. For the meaning you're on your own."

The cousins slouched onto their beds and thought. Minutes passed, in which all that could be heard was the gurgle of Tess' tummy and the ticking of several stumped brains.

Tess rolled over and propped herself up with her arms. "Does anyone know who G is?"

"It's got to be Gabriela," said Olivia.

"It could be Señor Gustavo," said Lissy.

"What about Grandma?" asked Aidan.

Tess' jaw dropped.

"Why would *they* be leaving notes in our room?" asked Cagney.

Lissy shook her head. "Why would anybody?"

"Hey! Do you remember when we were having breakfast?" Cagney sat up. "Aidan overheard Pietro and Gabriela talking about digging."

"They must have been talking about a dig," said Olivia.

"You mean with a bucket and spade?" asked Tess.

Aidan smiled. "Kind of. When people want to discover old things they say they are going on a dig."

"Mainly it's archaeologists and paleontologists," said Lissy.

"But they also have photographers," said Aidan.

Olivia bounded to her feet. "And who do we know who's a photographer and whose name begins with G?"

"Okay, so now we know it's Gabriela," said Cagney. "But that makes no sense. Why did she leave a clue for these pictures in our room?"

Lissy shook her head. "That's a bit more difficult."

"And now we've got them, who are we supposed to give them to?" asked Olivia.

"Yep," said Lissy. "Who *are* the right people?"

Suddenly the room plunged into darkness.

"Hey! Who turned off the lights?" asked Tess.

"Oh for goodness' sake," said Cagney. "Stop prattling about and turn them back on."

"It's not only the light," said Lissy. "Spider's died too."

"Then somebody open the curtains!" demanded Cagney.

Olivia felt her way through the darkness to the window. She flung open the curtains and light streamed into the room. Flinching at the sunlight she turned her back on the window.

Lissy perched on the bed, a worried look on her face. "Cagney, did you copy and paste those pictures or transfer them?"

"Transferred," said Cagney.

Lissy closed her eyes and winced. "I don't suppose you backed them up?"

"I thought you did," said Cagney. "You're the technical genius around here, not me."

Aidan placed a hand on Lissy's shoulder and she took a deep breath. Spider had only lost power once before and it hadn't been good. Files not saved were lost in the blink of an eye and almost impossible to get back. If Cagney had copied the pictures they would still be on the flashcard, but she hadn't copied them, she had transferred them. Lissy could have kicked herself for not paying more attention. The lights flickered on. With trembling fingers Lissy re-booted Spider and waited. Five minutes later she looked up. "They're gone!"

16

The Plan

Lissy's fingers flew across the keys.

"Oops!" said Tess.

"Oops is right," said Aidan.

"You can get them back, right Lissy?" asked Tess.

Lissy's voice was small, and cracked as she spoke. "I'm trying, but I think they've disappeared."

"This is a disaster," said Cagney.

Olivia's eyes grew bug-like. "Ya think!"

The cousins slumped onto Lissy's bed, stunned. Silence filled the room. The cousins had made mistakes before, but nothing like this. Important pictures, obviously destined for someone other than them, had been lost.

Cagney jumped to her feet. "There's nothing else for it." She pointed a finger at Lissy "*You* lost the pictures, so now we'll have to find the treasure and re-take them."

Lissy stared at her open-mouthed. "*I* lost the pictures?"

"I know," said Cagney. "But don't worry, we're not going to hold that against you. Anyone can make a mistake."

Lissy could barely get her words out. Her face turned puce as she sputtered to speak. "She's ... she's ... she's joking, right?"

Olivia bit her lip and tried not to laugh. Cagney wasn't known for joking and this didn't seem a particularly good moment for her to start.

"I think it's an excellent idea." Aidan winked at Lissy. "And your masterly plan is?"

Cagney plopped onto the bed. "Well, that's the tricky bit."

Lissy frowned. She shook her head. She didn't want to be any part of finding treasure, but a riddle had been discovered and she couldn't help herself. Lissy had never met a riddle she hadn't cracked. She slipped off the bed and paced the room. "Let's think about it logically. What do we know for sure?"

"We know you lost the pictures," stated Cagney.

"It wasn't me who lost the pictures," insisted Lissy. "It was the power cut."

"Excuses, excuses! You know, it's a poor workman who blames his fools!" said Cagney.

Aidan stifled a smile and tried to move the conversation on. "We know Gabriela took pictures of the treasure."

"We know she's left the hotel never to be seen again," said Cagney.

Lissy stopped mid pace. "Yes, that's a problem."

Tess sprung to her feet. "George Chavez!"

"George who?" said Olivia.

"That's what Pietro said when he got into the taxi," replied Tess.

The cousins looked at her dumbstruck. Aidan shook his head. "You're brilliant."

Tess wrinkled her nose. "Aw, shucks!"

"All we need to do is find out who George Chavez is," said Aidan. "And where he lives."

Lissy grabbed Spider off the bed and started a search.

"Easy peasy!" said Tess, pirouetting across the room.

"How many George Chavezes can there be in Lima?" said Aidan.

Lissy pressed enter and shook her head. "Three thousand four hundred and fifty two."

Olivia's eyes widened. "That's a set-back."

"Ya think!" said Cagney.

"Let's go and ask Señor Gustavo." Aidan scrambled off the bed. "Maybe he knows which George Chavez it is."

The cousins rushed along the hallway and down the dusty staircase. Señor Gustavo was polishing his nameplate. He turned, beaming, to face the cousins.

"My leetle Puddelitos. How can Señor Gustavo be of assistance?"

The cousins came to a skidding halt in front of him.

Cagney cleared her throat and put on her sweetest smile. "Do you know a George Chavez?"

"Not personally," replied Señor Gustavo.

"But you've heard of him?" asked Olivia.

"Oh yes, everyone knows him. He is very famous."

Lissy sighed in relief. "Can you tell us where he lives?"

"Not exactly." Señor Gustavo gave Lissy a sympathetic look. "Unfortunately, he is dead."

"Dead?" gasped Cagney.

"Yes, he died in 1910 trying to cross the Alps."

Aidan scratched his head. "He was trying to walk across the Alps?"

"Not walk," explained Señor Gustavo. "Fly. Our airport is named in his honor. Jorge Chavez International Airport."

The cousins wandered into the courtyard and sank into the old wicker chairs.

"They were going to the airport," said Olivia.

Lissy let out a deep sigh. "Of course. It's obvious now."

"They could be anywhere." Cagney folded her arms across her chest. "Let's face it, we're never going to find them."

Lissy shook her head. She was not going to give up that easily. "Do you think they might have gone back to the dig?"

Aidan shrugged. "I guess."

"But how do we find out where the dig is?" asked Tess.

Cagney snatched a magazine off the table. "It's hopeless; I could have told you this was a hair-brained scheme from the beginning."

Olivia scowled. "It was *your* hair-brained scheme!"

Cagney chose to ignore this and flicked a page.

Lissy leapt to her feet. "I've got it! Do you remember when we checked in, Señor Gustavo asked Aidan to sign the guest book?"

"That's right!" Aidan stood so quickly his chair toppled backwards. "I had to give my name, address and phone number."

"If we take a look at the guest book, we can see where Gabriela and Pietro come from," said Lissy.

The cousins sped back into the lobby. Señor Gustavo was behind the desk doing what could only be described as a kind of mambo: as he spun around, the cousins were astonished to see a feather duster clamped between his teeth. Señor Gustavo whisked the feather duster out of his mouth and hid it behind his quivering belly. Pulling a stray curl behind his ear he raised an inquiring eyebrow.

Lissy giggled. A warning look from Cagney made her step back and clamp a hand over her mouth. Cagney pushed the thought of Señor Gustavo dancing the mambo out of her head and donned her serious look. It was a look grown-ups loved; a look that never failed.

"Would it be at all possible to see the guest book, please?" Cagney said, sweetly.

Señor Gustavo's arm reappeared from behind his back. He dropped the feather duster out of sight, and reaching across the desk, put a large, sausage-like finger on top of a red leather book.

Slowly, he shook his head. "I am sorry Puddelitos, but it is private. I cannot be showing just anyone."

"But we're not just anyone," said Aidan. "We're the fabulous Callie Puddleton's grandchildren. Remember?"

Señor Gustavo grasped the guest book and placed it under the counter. "I am sorry," he said, "but no."

"But ..." said Olivia.

"No buts." Señor Gustavo wagged his finger. "Now, go enjoy the beautiful Peruvian day."

Picking up his feather duster he shooed the cousins towards the courtyard. They were half way across the lobby when the door flew open and Cook hurtled in. The cousins scattered as she barged through them and approached the desk.

"Señor Gustavo, Señor Gustavo! It is Santiago. He has placed a small coin from the Sapo game up his nose."

Senior Gustavo's smile disappeared as quickly as a plate full of donuts in front of Tess. "*Ese niño tonto*! But do not fear, Cook. Señor Gustavo will get the coin out. Come."

The cousins watched as Señor Gustavo squeezed himself from behind the desk and waddled like an anxious duck across the lobby. As soon as the door swung closed, Olivia scampered towards the desk, leapt over it, and pulled out the guest book.

"Keep watch," she said, flicking through the large red book. "Here's Aidan's name. Pietro must be right after him."

The situation in the courtyard was comical to watch, but it still didn't stop Lissy's heart from racing at twice the normal speed.

"Quick!" shouted Cagney. "Señor Gustavo's almost got the coin."

Tess tilted her head to the side. "Do you think it's okay to hold someone upside down and shake them?"

"It seems to have worked." Aidan grimaced. "Wow, look at the slime on that."

"Uuurrrgh!" Cagney turned her back on the courtyard and wafted the air in front of her face. "That's disgusting."

"Poor Santiago," said Lissy.

"One more minute." Olivia continued to flick through the book. "I have to find Gabriela."

"He's coming," said Aidan.

"Do something!" cried Lissy.

Señor Gustavo threw open the doors and Tess fainted in his arms.

17

The Nazca Lines

Tess brushed down her pink tulle skirt.

"You're getting scarily good at that," said Aidan.

Tess grinned. "I am, aren't I?"

Señor Gustavo had carried Tess upstairs and gently laid her on the bed. Some ancient smelling salts had been produced and, after several glasses of water, Señor Gustavo had at last been convinced Tess was not going to die. Ten minutes later he left the room.

"So?" said Cagney. "What did the guest book *say?*"

Olivia smiled. "Looks like we're going to Machu Picchu after all."

The cousins waited on the steps outside Hotel Miserias. A blast of horn and screech of tires alerted the cousins to Lucila's approach.

Juddering to a stop, Lucila beckoned the cousins. "Jump in."

The cousins threw their bags in the trunk and clambered inside.

"If our grandma arrives," said Lissy. "Will you please tell her we'll return in a few days."

"Everything is taken care of." Lucila flashed a golden smile. "You will be in the safe hands. Now hurry. Your plane awaits."

The airport, where Emilio's plane lived, was much smaller than Jorge Chavez. It was in the middle of nowhere, and possessed one building whose appearance was less like a terminal – more like a hut. A single, black-clad arm waved out the small grubby window, as Lucila hurtled past, weaving across the cracked tarmac, speeding toward a tiny red plane.

Emilio was already behind the controls and he gave a brisk military salute as Lucila and her rolling aquarium spluttered to a stop.

Tess flapped her pink fuzzy scarf in response and bounded onto the airstrip. Tess had decided she loved to fly. As her lifelong dream of becoming a fairy had recently been squashed by a lack of developing wings, she had decided instead, that the life of a pilot might be a good substitute.

Aidan was not quite as enamored. He slowly emerged from the jeep and studied the plane. It didn't take very long; there was very little of it. Aidan had seen cars bigger than Emilio's plane. Heck, he'd seen beds bigger. "*That's* what we're flying in?" he asked, trying not to let his voice shake.

"*Si*," said Lucila. "Don't worry, it is quite safe. It has never crashed."

Aidan took a deep breath. "That's reassuring."

"Well, not recently anyway," added Lucila.

Aidan stared at her in horror.

"I am joking, leetle Puddleton." Lucila slapped Aidan on the back. "You have nothing to worry about. My sweet Emilio flies *almost* as well as I drive."

Aidan gulped as the remaining color drained from his pale face.

Lucila drew Aidan towards her in a bear hug. "Do not worry, little Puddleton. You will be quite safe."

The cousins clambered into the plane, buckled themselves in and prepared for take-off. The plane really *was* tiny. In fact, it was so tiny, Tess had to sit up front with Emilio.

"Do you really think we should let Tess sit so close to all those knobs and switches?" whispered Aidan.

"Don't worry about me," said Tess, "I'll be fine."

Cagney rolled her eyes. "It wasn't *you* we were worried about."

Lissy placed her hand on Tess' shoulder. "Just don't touch anything, okay Tess?"

"I won't, but what's that?" Tess pointed towards a large red button.

"Don't!" yelled the cousins.

Tess grinned at Emilio. "Just joking!"

Emilio finished his checks, shoved his logbook under his seat and fastened his seat belt. "Are you ready?"

Aidan's mumbled 'no' was drowned out by a resounding 'yes'.

Emilio smiled. "Then Machu Picchu, here we come."

The plane bumped along the runway, tilted back and climbed into the pale blue sky.

Olivia craned her neck to peer out the window. "Hey guys, look down there."

"Who's that talking to Lucila?" asked Lissy.

"Tess, you have the best view," shouted Cagney. "Who's getting in the jeep with her?"

"I'm not 100% sure," said Tess, her button nose squished against the window, "but it looks a lot like our friend, Sneezy."

The countryside surrounding Lima was stunning. With the ocean to their right and the dry, dusty desert stretching ahead, Aidan soon forgot how scared he was and concentrated instead on not losing his breakfast.

An hour into the flight Emilio scooted around, a wide grin on his face. "I have a surprise for you."

"Ooh! I love surprises." Tess clapped her hands. "Is it an ice-cream sundae?"

"No." Emilio laughed. "It is better than an ice-cream sundae. I have taken the liberty of going on a slight detour. Look below."

Emilio tilted the plane to the right. The five peered out the windows. Hundreds of feet below were intricate lines carved into the soil.

"There's a monkey with a big curly tail." Tess squeaked with delight.

"And a bird!" cried Lissy, whose middle name was Bird, and loved all things feathered.

"So? It's just a bunch of drawings," said Cagney.

"To be precise," said Emilio, "three hundred drawings. All of them etched into the desert sand."

Cagney took out her camera and snapped a couple of pictures. "I guess it *is* pretty cool."

"What are they doing out here?" asked Olivia.

Emilio shrugged. "No one knows."

"They seem to go on forever," said Aidan, who was trying to stare at the horizon and not at a bobble-headed man who had just come into view.

"They cover over 250 square miles," explained Emilio.

"What are they called?" asked Tess.

"The Nazca Lines."

Olivia looked confused. "I thought that was something to do with race cars."

Emilio smiled. "Not NASCAR, Nazca," he said. "Ancient lines."

Tess wrinkled her nose. "But who drew them?"

"We think they were created by the people of the Nazca civilization," said Emilio. "But no one who drew them ever saw them."

"Why on earth not?" asked Cagney.

"Fifteen hundred years ago they didn't have planes. The only way to see the Nazca Lines is from above. On the ground you can't tell what they are."

Olivia narrowed her eyes. "So how did they draw them if they couldn't see them?"

"That's the mystery." Emilio's eyebrows rose. "Some people have suggested the lines could be the world's largest astronomy calendar. Others say they were drawn to help alien space ships land."

Aidan and Olivia stared at each other. "Cool!"

"What do you think?" asked Olivia.

Emilio shrugged. "I think we will never know."

The cousins fell silent as the plane drifted over the artwork made of soil. Peru was such a wonderful country.

Full of friendly people, thought Lissy.

Full of fabulous treasure, thought Cagney.

Full of ancient mystery, thought Aidan.

Emilio flew the plane back and forth across The Lines, tipping the wings and diving to get a closer look. Aidan shut his eyes and breathed deeply. He had been on roller coasters worse than this, but roller coasters were anchored to the ground. Now he thought about it, he'd thrown up on those too. Finally, the plane leveled off. Aidan opened his eyes and his mouth dropped. The ground below was no longer flat; it soared towards the clouds.

Aidan gasped. "Those hills … they're stunning."

"Not hills," said Emilio. "Mountains. The Andean Mountains."

"My goodness. They're beautiful." Lissy gazed at the snowcapped peaks in the distance.

"The Andes are almost four-and-a-half-thousand miles long," said Emilio.

"Whoa!" said Olivia, "that's one heck of a hike."

"They run through seven countries and are over 300 miles wide in places."

"They're the tallest mountain range, right?" asked Tess.

"No," said Emilio, "but they are the longest."

Aidan felt the plane drop and clamped both hands over his mouth. A drop of sweat trickled down his back. "Is that where we're going?" he mumbled.

"We are going to Cuzco," Emilio replied. "The Capital of the Inca Empire."

18

Up in the Clouds

Twenty minutes later Emilio touched down in Cuzco. He guided the plane towards a small hanger and parked. The cousins scrambled out and threw their backpacks over their shoulders. Emilio followed, and escorted the five to a sleek looking car sitting on the runway.

"This car will take you to the train station," said Emilio. "Once you reach Machu Picchu you have reservations at the Cloud Hotel."

"We do?" Aidan gulped in the fresh mountain air, his face a delicate shade of Kermit.

Emilio smiled. "Of course."

Cagney started towards the long black car, a smile at her lips. "I guess if we have to rough it, we have to rough it. As I always say, beggars can't be losers."

"Don't forget to say hi to Callie for me." Emilio turned and strolled towards the plane. "Get her to tell you the joke about the noodle and the tea-pot," he said laughing.

"Grandma's here?" yelled Olivia.

Emilio climbed into the plane. "I thought you knew," he said puzzled. "I flew her in late yesterday."

The cousins waved goodbye and joined Cagney in the waiting car. An imposing figure wearing a chauffeur's cap nodded curtly, put the car in gear, and glided across the tarmac.

"I'm so excited," said Lissy. "I can't believe Grandma's here."

Olivia shook her head. "That woman sure gets around."

"Yeah," said Cagney," except it would be nice if she got around with us."

"I wonder why she came to Machu Picchu without us?" asked Aidan.

Olivia shrugged. "I wonder why Grandma does a lot of things."

"Do you think she'll be mad at us for leaving the hotel?" asked Tess.

Lissy went pale. "Oh dear, I hadn't thought of that."

"She was really mad when Olivia broke Mrs. Snoops' window with a crab apple," said Tess. "Do you think flying on a plane without her across Peru is better or worse than breaking Mrs. Snoops' window?"

Cagney rolled her eyes. "What do you think?"

Tess rubbed the end of her nose. "I think we're toast."

The car meandered through the cobbled streets of Cuzco. Under crystal blue skies the car passed white-washed buildings until it drew alongside the station. The cousins jumped out. Slinging their bags over their shoulders, they bounded up the steps and through the doors. They skidded to a stop by a small opening in the wall.

Aidan took a deep breath and in his best Spanish asked for five tickets to Machu Picchu. Aidan didn't mind talking in Spanish; he was getting quite fluent. What he was worried about was being questioned as to why they were traveling without an adult. Aidan held his breath, but the young lady issuing the tickets seemed to have no interest in why the five were alone and, with a wide smile, pushed the tickets towards him.

As soon as the cousins boarded, the bright blue train lurched forward and started its journey south. Soon the terracotta roofs of Cuzco faded into memory, replaced by lush green countryside.

"Is that a llama?" asked Tess.

Lissy peered through the train window. "I think it's an alpaca. But I could be wrong."

"How do you know the difference?" asked Aidan, who had finally turned a more healthy shade of pink.

"The size," replied Lissy. "A llama is twice as big as an alpaca and can weigh up to 280 pounds.

"Maybe it's a baby llama," said Tess. "Hello, Cuddles!" she yelled through the window.

The train descended from Cuzco. Hugging the mountainside, it swished into the valley and began to follow the wiggling Urubamba River. Aidan's nose pressed so close to the window, the glass started to steam. He wiped away the condensation and scooched into his seat. "So, what's our plan of action?"

"What, you mean if Grandma hasn't grounded us for life?" asked Lissy.

Cagney slipped into her seat and pushed her uneven glasses onto the bridge of her nose. "It's easy. We'll find the treasure, take the pictures, and return to Lima pronto."

"A simple plan," said Olivia. "I like it."

"Me too," muttered Tess, her mouth full of candy.

"Hand them over Tess." Aidan reached for the bag. "I'm starving."

"Sure," said Tess.

The cousins un-wrapped the candy Tess had bought by-the-pound from a street vendor at the station.

Cagney pressed her cheek up against the window. "Are we there yet?"

Lissy raised her eyebrows. "Not yet. Spider says it takes three hours to get to the town of Aguas Calientes. Then a bus takes you to the top of the mountain."

"How did they ever discover this place?" asked Aidan. "It's a jungle out there."

Lissy turned Spider around for the cousins to see and read aloud. "Machu Picchu was discovered in 1911 by a U.S. Senator named Hiram Bingham. He was actually searching for the lost city of Vilcabamba, but after trekking along the banks of the Urubamba River and climbing a mountain covered in dense jungle, he found Machu Picchu instead."

"He sounds very brave," said Tess.

Cagney sniffed. "He sounds crazy."

"Actually, Cagney's right. Spider says the most dangerous snake in South America lives in this part of the world. The fer-de-lance can kill you with one bite."

"Yowza!" said Tess.

Olivia settled into her seat and shoved her feet onto Lissy's lap. "You know, I like Hiss, but I don't think I want to meet a fer-de-lance."

The train chugged into Aguas Calientes. The cousins ignored the tumbledown row of market stalls and headed straight towards the bus. It took only another thirty minutes of zigzagging up a perilous dirt track before the cousins scuttled off the bus and clambered up the stone steps into the aptly named Cloud Hotel.

The hotel was everything Hotel Miserias was not. It was busy, it was opulent and it felt a long way from home. The cousins hurried across the vast marble lobby and came to a stop under a sparkling chandelier. A plump, pompous-looking man stood behind the desk. His nametag said Octavio. Lissy peered at him. He reminded her of Danny DeVito, but without the hair, without the height and without the sense of humor.

Octavio peered over the desk at the cousins. "Welcome to the Cloud Hotel. How may I be of assistance?"

Cagney felt a hand in the small of her back as she was propelled forward. "Er, we have a reservation for Puddleton," she sputtered.

"And you are?" Octavio cocked an eyebrow.

"We're the Smiths." Aidan was still pale from the trek up the mountain. The over crowded bus, hairpin turns and sheer drops had done nothing to help his stomach, and he was feeling unusually petulant. Never again would he complain about catching the school bus. Never again would he complain about any form of American transportation. Nothing could ever be as bad as what he'd just experienced; even riding shotgun with Lucila paled in comparison.

Cagney gave him a withering look. Aidan moved his feet quickly and took a step back.

"He's joking," she explained to the un-amused Octavio.

Lissy stepped forward and smiled sweetly. "Sir, *we're* the Puddletons."

"And you are traveling with?" asked Octavio.

"Ooh, ooh, I know," said Tess. "Our grandma, *Callie* Puddleton."

Octavio sniffed. "Oh, yes, the infamous Callie Puddleton."

Tess frowned. "She's famous?"

"*Si*. Never have we had a guest receive so many phone calls in such a short time."

"Phone calls?" Cagney shook her head. "Very hard to imagine."

"Yes, 36 to be exact." Octavio pulled out a green spotted handkerchief and dabbed his forehead. "All in the middle of the night."

"She's *very* popular," said Lissy.

"So it would seem," said Octavio. "So, where *is* your grandma?"

"Where *is* she?" asked Aidan.

"Yes, where is she," repeated Octavio. He bounced on his tippy-toes. "No one has seen her since she checked in. She even missed her free breakfast. No one misses the free breakfast. It is a very good breakfast."

The cousins looked at each other dumbstruck.

"We're not sure–" began Lissy.

Cagney gave her a nudge. "What my cousin is trying to say–"

"Is she's sick," blurted Olivia. She looked at the others for help.

"Oh yeah, serious grandma problems." Tess gripped her non-existent tummy and gave it a good shake.

Aidan rolled his eyes. "Believe me, you don't want to know."

Tess started humming 'Twinkle Twinkle Little Star' with tooting noises. Cagney flashed her a look. Tess changed the song to 'I'm a Yankee Doodle Dandy'. Cagney clapped her hand in front of Tess' mouth.

Lissy stifled a laugh. "In fact she told us to get our key, some Pepto Bismol and come straight up."

"Hmmm!" Octavio's eyebrows furrowed as he dangled the key in front of them. Listen boy-"

Olivia reached up and grabbed it. "Thanks."

The cousins turned and fled.

The five were half way across the lobby when Aidan stopped. "Rats! We forgot to ask about Gabriela."

"I'll take care of it." Cagney turned back. "Excuse me, sir, could you tell us if a couple named Gabriela and Pietro are staying at this hotel?"

"Hmmm?" Octavio once again bounced up and down on his tippy-toes. "Señorita Castilla and Señor Ponti stay here often while they are working at the dig."

"Really!" Tess clapped her hands together. "How exciting."

"Hmmm." Octavio shrugged his shoulders. "Not really. The dig has not been a huge success. They have only found a few clay pots. However, this happens sometimes."

Tess wrinkled her nose. "But what about the treasure?"

"Treasure?" Octavio's lopsided smile broke into a laugh. "Unfortunately," he said, turning his back, "this time, there is no treasure."

The cousins found their room. Tumbling inside, Aidan slammed the door behind them.

"So that's it." Cagney paced back and forth. "They've found the treasure and they're not telling anyone."

"Is that legal?" asked Tess.

"It most definitely is not," said Aidan.

Lissy clambered onto the nearest bed. "No wonder Gabriela wanted to show someone those pictures."

"She had proof they'd discovered the treasure," said Aidan.

Tess nodded. "I bet that nasty old Pietro was trying to keep it a secret."

"It doesn't explain why she was leaving the clues in our room though," said Olivia.

"It doesn't explain why Grandma's missing," said Lissy.

"One thing at a time," said Cagney. "At least we're getting closer to the truth."

"Now, if we could just get to the dig and take pictures of the treasure without anyone seeing us," said Olivia.

"Could we eat first?" asked Tess.

Lissy marveled how Tess could remain so thin. The amount she ate, Tess should weigh as much as all of them put together. But Tess was thin, stick thin. Lissy shook her head; genetics – it just wasn't fair. She scooted off the bed and held out her hand. "Come on then."

19

Machu Picchu

The cousins slept until the sun peeked through their window. Tess sat up and rubbed her eyes. She surveyed the scene. Next to her Olivia lay, mouth wide-open, arms above her head. Across the room, Lissy's head was stuffed under a pillow, and Cagney resembled the dead – flat on her back, blankets up to her chin, arms folded across her chest. Tess searched the room for Aidan. Finally she spied him, a tangled mess of blankets and pillows on the floor. Tess' eyes moved toward the door, under which a note had been slipped.

"Ooh look! We've got mail."

Aidan opened one eye, slowly followed by the other. Rising to his knees, he inched his way across the floor and scooped up the note. "It's from Grandma."

Lissy pulled the pillow off her head and stretched. "Is she mad at us?"

Aidan shrugged. "It depends what she means by the words 'grounded for life'."

"Yep, she's mad," said Olivia.

"It says she'll return tomorrow and if we leave Machu Picchu before she gets back, she'll … well, you probably don't want to know what she says." Aidan folded the letter and shoved it into the pocket of his shorts.

Olivia made a lunge for the note. "Come on Aidan, how bad can it be?"

Aidan shook his head. "Do you remember how mad Grandma was when you planted sprouts on her living room rug?"

Olivia winced. Within a week of the planting, Grandma Callie had a harvest of bean sprouts all over her newly carpeted floors. "And this is worse?"

Aidan nodded. "Way worse."

Olivia slid off the bed and trotted towards the bathroom. "Yep, then it's definitely best you keep it to yourself."

Lissy slung her feet over the side of the bed and wiggled them into her slippers. "So are we going to forget the plan?"

The others looked shocked.

"We can't give up now," said Aidan. "Besides, Grandma didn't say anything about finding the treasure."

"Grandma doesn't know about the treasure," Lissy pointed out.

"Details!" shouted Olivia from the bathroom.

Aidan nodded. "All Grandma said was we have to stay on Machu Picchu."

"Exactly," said Cagney. "It's a pretty big place. What are we going to do, fall off?"

The cousins threw on their clothes and headed downstairs. Reaching the door to the restaurant, Cagney stopped. "Oh great. What do we say if we see Gabriela and Pietro at breakfast?"

"Smile." Tess pushed open the door. "I find that normally works."

"Aren't they going to think it strange we're here?" Aidan held the door for the others.

Lissy followed Tess into the restaurant. "Not really. Machu Picchu is the most visited tourist site in Peru. It makes perfect sense we'd be here."

Lissy was right. The restaurant buzzed with tourists. Every person seemed to have a camera around their neck, and a guidebook in their hands. The cousins wandered through the restaurant listening to the varying voices of people from countries all over the world. They reached an empty table and dropped into their seats.

"I don't see them," said Olivia.

"Me neither," said Lissy.

Aidan stood and gazed around the busy restaurant. "Pietro's blond hair should make him easy to spot."

Tess grabbed a bread roll and stuffed half of it into her mouth. "He's probably still in bed, lazy so-and-so."

"Or they've left," said Cagney.

"No, don't say that," said Lissy. "We *have* to find them."

"Look," said Tess, waving frantically, "there's Gabriela."

Gabriela spotted Tess across the dining room. A large smile lit her face as she dashed towards her. "I did not expect to see you here. Your grandma? She is with you?"

"Not exactly," said Cagney. "She got here yesterday, but she seems to be missing... again."

"You mean, you haven't seen her either?" asked Lissy.

"What?" said Gabriela. "I had no idea she was here." Gabriela sunk into an empty chair and closed her eyes.

"Did you hide that note for Grandma?" blurted Olivia.

Gabriela's eyes opened wide. Her mocha skin paled. She slapped the palm of her hand on her forehead and sighed deeply.

"It's no good denying it," said Cagney. "Olivia found the note."

"And Aidan found the flash card," said Lissy.

Gabriela took a deep breath.

"Gabriela!" Pietro's raspy voice boomed across the restaurant.

Tess jumped at least a foot in the air.

Gabriela stood and gave Tess a hug. "I can't talk now. Meet me at the Sun Temple in an hour. I will explain everything."

The cousins ate a hasty breakfast and dashed outside into the sun.

Tess placed her arms above her head and stretched. "It's so nice to see the sun again. My pink fuzzy hair bands were getting quite depressed in all that fog."

Cagney snorted. "Which way to the ruins?"

Aidan shrugged. "I guess we could just follow the crowd."

"Or the map." Tess pulled a guidebook from beneath her poncho and tossed it to Lissy.

"Yeah, that helps," said Olivia.

The cousins ambled along the path away from the hotel. They rounded a bend and stopped dead. There, below them, lay the Lost City of Machu Picchu. Row after row of stone terraces were built into the side of a mountaintop so steep, it was a wonder the buildings didn't slide off. The five gazed at the panoramic view. Aidan had once seen a picture of Yosemite in a National Geographic magazine. He imagined this was what it felt like to stand on the tallest peak in Yosemite – except better.

"Wow!" said Aidan. "That's incredible. How on earth did they get those rocks up here?"

"No one knows for sure," Lissy said, reading the guidebook. "They think hundreds of men pushed them up the mountain."

"Right!" Cagney snapped a couple of pictures. "That's impossible."

Aidan looked around at the clusters of buildings. "Apparently not."

The cousins walked through the ruined city, mesmerized by its beauty.

"Here," said Lissy. "According to the map this is the Temple of the Sun. This is where Gabriela said she'd meet us."

The five entered a round tower. In the center lay a carved rock. Several tiny square windows dotted the thick stone walls.

Lissy perched on a ledge and read aloud. "During the summer and winter solstices the edge of the rock is highlighted by the sun coming through one of the windows."

Aidan scratched his head. "But how could they figure *that* out?"

Lissy shrugged. "I don't know, but they did."

Aidan traced his fingers across the wall. "These rocks are amazing. They fit together so well."

"Also, the Inca didn't use mortar." Lissy looked up from the guidebook. "All these rocks are carved to fit together perfectly. The city was built 500 years ago by the best stone masons the world has ever known."

"I am glad you like our Lost City." Gabriela appeared from behind the circular wall.

The cousins spun around at the sound of her voice. "It was built in 1450 by the Inca. It is one of the few places the Spanish did not destroy when they came to Peru."

"Why didn't they destroy it?" asked Aidan.

Gabriela winked. "They couldn't find it."

"But why is it built on top of a mountain?" asked Olivia.

Gabriela swept her dark hair over her shoulder and smiled. "Some people say it was a fortress. Others think the Inca royalty lived here in the summer."

"Machu Picchu," said Tess, rolling the words around in her mouth. "It sure is a funny name."

"It means 'Old Mountain'. If you look over there you will see Huayna Picchu, which means 'Young Mountain'." Gabriela pointed at a vast rock towering over them like a rocket ship.

"It's stunning," said Aidan.

"Legend says Huayna Picchu was why the Inca built their city here. It is the nose of the city. This means the Inca rulers are lying down and forever gazing towards the Gods."

"So basically we're looking up the nose of an Inca King," said Aidan.

Cagney gave him a look and Aidan went scarlet. Gabriela laughed.

"How do you know all these things about the Inca?" asked Lissy, changing the subject. "Did they leave books?"

Gabriela shook her head. "There were no books. The Inca had no written language."

"I knew it," said Olivia. "I've always said learning to write is way overrated."

"Let's walk," said Gabriela. "I will tell you more about Machu Picchu and everything about the treasure."

*
* *

20

Gabriela Tells All

The cousins followed Gabriela out of the Sun Temple. They strolled across the ruins, past llamas happily nibbling at the grass, past tourists wielding their cameras. No matter which direction they looked the panorama was beyond stunning; it was breathtaking.

Olivia squinted against the fierce sun and rubbed her temple. Something was not right. Olivia had not been sick her entire life; she was darned if she was going to start now. But something was pressing down on her head. Something Olivia had never felt before.

Lissy stopped and looked back. "Are you okay, Olivia?"

Olivia squeezed her eyes shut and clutched her head. She caught up with the others and winced. "I'm sorry guys, my head feels all dizzy."

Gabriela ruffled Olivia's black hair. "I'm not surprised. Machu Picchu is almost 8,000 feet above sea-level. It is not unusual to have altitude sickness at this height."

"I don't have altitude sickness." Olivia clutched her head as another wave of nausea hit her. "I never get sick."

Gabriela gave her a squeeze. "Not even *you* can fight altitude sickness." She handed Olivia a bottle of water. "Here, drink this. Water helps."

Olivia took the bottle and slugged a few gulps. She looked up expectantly. "Nope. Head still hurts."

"It will hurt, probably for several hours," explained Gabriela. "Unfortunately it takes more than a few sips of water. Keep drinking, but if you are not better by tomorrow you should go down into the valley."

Aidan glanced around. He felt like he was on top of the world, and it turned out they weren't far off. "Wow, we *are* high."

"Yes," said Gabriela. "Machu Picchu sits on a cliff between two mountains. Two thousand feet below us is the Urubamba River."

Gabriela linked her arm through Olivia's and continued walking. Olivia stiffened. She wasn't too sure about being manhandled by a stranger. What did Gabriela think she was, a toddler? Olivia was about to say something when a searing pain wracked her head. Olivia grabbed on tightly to Gabriela's arm and decided not to complain.

"Ma'am, how long did the Inca live here?" asked Lissy.

"Only about a hundred years," said Gabriela. "And then it was abandoned."

"Ooh, that's sad." Tess gazed around at the hundreds of ruins. "But why was it abandoned?"

"No one knows," said Gabriela. "It is one of Peru's many mysteries."

"Speaking of mysteries," Cagney stopped and turned to face Gabriela, "would you please explain what's going on?"

Gabriela's face clouded. "Yes. I think you have earned that right."

Gabriela sank onto the edge of a terrace. The cousins gathered around her and listened.

"I met Pietro six months ago while staying at Hotel Miserias. He is an archeologist, a treasure hunter. He asked me to visit the dig he was working on. He was convinced there was great treasure in the jungle close to Machu Picchu. A couple of weeks later, he struck gold. He rushed to Lima to tell the authorities. While he was gone I took many pictures of the treasure."

"So they *were* your pictures," said Lissy.

Gabriela held up a hand and nodded. "But when Pietro returned, he had changed. He told me we were going to take the treasure secretly to Lima. He was so scared it would get stolen, he forbade me to tell anyone. But I didn't believe him. One day, I overheard him talking to one of the workers. He was planning to steal it all. He hadn't told the government in Lima. Instead, he met with several bad men. Men who would pay anything to get their hands on the gold. The next day I got away and flew to Lima."

"Whoa!" said Olivia, clutching her head, "that's major."

Gabriela's voice shrunk to a whisper. "I knew your grandma. We met at the Hotel Miserias many years ago. So I called her, explained what was happening and she said she would come."

"Grandma?" exclaimed Lissy.

"Sssh." Gabriela checked over her shoulder.

"Our grandma?" whispered Tess.

Gabriela nodded.

"But how do you know Grandma? How on earth did you even meet her?" asked Aidan.

Gabriela let out a long sigh and slowly shook her head. "There are some things I am unable to tell you, my little ones. Let us just say for now that we met."

Olivia ran a hand through her short black hair. "But why didn't you go to the police?"

"I was sure Pietro was having me followed. I didn't dare chance it. I waited for two days and then you arrived without her. I was confused. Then Pietro came to Lima. You saw him arrive at the hotel. He was so angry. I told him I had been sick and needed to go to a doctor. He was not convinced, but it gave me time to think of a plan."

"Ooh! I like plans," said Tess.

Gabriela smiled weakly. "Room 24 was where your grandma stayed before. I remembered she had shown me a secret hiding place there. I decided to hide a clue in case I wasn't there when she arrived. I knew she would remember the hiding place. I didn't dare hide the compact flash, in case you found it. Also, when I first met Pietro, I made the mistake of telling him about this secret chamber."

"But he couldn't find it," said Aidan.

"All he did was stub his toe on the bottom of my bed," said Cagney.

"No, I never told him where it was, only that there was one. I felt sure that even if you or Pietro found the hiding place, you would not be able to figure out the clue. I guess I was wrong."

"Oh it was easy." Cagney took off her glasses and gave them a polish. Suddenly she noticed Lissy's expression. "Although, I guess we did have one or two false starts," she added.

"But Gabriela," said Lissy, softly. "I'm afraid we have bad news."

"Aidan studied his feet. "You're not going to be very happy."

"In fact, you'd better sit down," said Tess, patting the grass.

Gabriela frowned. "I am sitting down."

"Then maybe you should lie back," said Tess.

Gabriela gazed at the cousins in confusion. There was silence.

"Lissy lost the pictures," blurted Cagney.

Lissy hung her head and made a mental note to personally strangle Cagney when she got her alone.

Gabriela slumped forward and placed her head in her hands. "Oh no. What happened?"

"Power failure," explained Aidan, sheepishly.

Lissy put her arm around Gabriela's shoulder. "I am so, so sorry."

"But this was my only hope. I can't stop him by myself. I need proof. Now Pietro is suspicious, I will never get a chance to take the pictures again. Oh, I wish your grandma was here."

"But she's not," said Aidan.

"And we are," said Olivia. "In fact, that's why we came here."

"What do you mean?" asked Gabriela.

"We're going to re-take the pictures." Cagney looked up and beamed. Waving her arms confidently she declared. "Remember, if the fountain won't come to Mohammed, then Mohammed must go to the fountain."

Gabriela looked confused and her brows furrowed, but she let it go. "But you can't. You'll never find the dig by yourselves. It is hidden deep in the jungle and is almost impossible to find."

Aidan looked at Gabriela sheepishly. "Not by ourselves, but you could take us."

Gabriela shook her head. "I can't. Pietro would not allow it. Besides, we are leaving to go there this afternoon. I could never get you there and back in time."

"Well then," said Olivia. "We'll just have to follow you."

21

The Problem with Olivia

The cousins strolled with Gabriela in and out of stone buildings with high walls and steep open air roofs. Gabriela showed them the Temple of the Condor, the Sacred Rock and finally the Main Plaza. The tour complete, the cousins lay on the ground and gazed at the cloudless sky.

Gabriela perched beside them and sighed. "I really don't know how it would be possible for you to follow us."

"But ma'am, we're very small," said Lissy.

Tess kicked off her pink sparkly sneakers and gave her feet a rub. "And we're very quiet."

Everyone stared at Tess.

"Why are you looking at me?" asked Tess, looking hurt. "I can be quiet."

Gabriela frowned. "You have proved yourselves very resourceful. Maybe it is possible. But the trail is not easy. There is a lot of climbing and the path is very narrow, with steep drops. The jungle can be deadly, especially at night."

Cagney gulped. Steep drops were something she did not want to think about. Correction: she didn't mind thinking about them, she just didn't want to think about falling off them.

Aidan scratched his head. "Is the dig in Machu Picchu?"

Gabriela looked confused. "I don't think it has a name. The dig is in the interior of the jungle, nestled in the shadow of the mountain. Does it make a difference?"

"Trust us," said Olivia, remembering Grandma's note. "It makes a huge difference."

"If it has no name," reasoned Aidan, "then it's not really *not* Machu Picchu."

"That's a double negative," said Lissy.

Aidan shrugged. "It's all I've got."

"I say we go for it," said Lissy, with a sudden burst of confidence. "We can do it. I know we can."

"Besides it was—" Cagney stopped and looked at Lissy. She regrouped. "It was *us* who lost the pictures. We have to replace them."

Lissy offered her cousin a weak smile.

Gabriela shrugged. "All right. You can try. I will draw you a map and leave it at the reception desk. If you get lost, at least you will be able to find your way back."

"Sounds great." Aidan grinned. "I'm good at reading maps."

"When we get to the dig I will take Pietro into one of the huts. You only need a few seconds to take a couple of pictures. Once you have the pictures, return to the hotel and wait for your grandma. She will know what to do."

"We'll give you a head start," said Aidan. "We can follow at a distance. If Pietro looks back we'll hide behind the trees."

Tess flung herself backwards and kicked her pink stripey socks into the air. "Let Pietro go first. Then if he looks round he'll just see you."

Gabriela smiled. "I don't know if it's going to work. But if he does see you, turn and run. He has a horrible temper."

The cousins returned to the Cloud Hotel for lunch. Olivia pushed her chair from the table and rubbed her eyes. Her glass stood empty, but her food lay untouched.

Lissy looked at the plate piled high with food. Olivia was normally a good eater. Of course she paled in comparison to Tess, but Tess was a professional.

Lissy reached out and touched her cousin's arm. "Olivia, you've hardly chewed a thing."

Olivia grimaced. "It's this stupid headache. I guess I still have altitude sickness."

Cagney clattered her silverware onto her plate and looked serious. "Olivia, I think you should stay at the hotel."

"What?" said the others in unison.

The thought of doing this without Olivia was incomprehensible. Olivia was the brave one. Olivia was the daring one. Olivia dragged a hand through her hair and let out a sigh of relief.

Cagney held up a hand. "Gabriela is leaving us a map. How hard can it be? They're leaving at one; Gabriela says we'll be back by five, six at the latest."

Olivia frowned. "You can't go alone."

"I'll go with you, sis. Mom and Dad would have a fit if I let you go into the jungle by yourself."

Cagney laughed. "I think our parents are way past throwing a fit. We're not going to be grounded, we're going to be stomped into it. We're going to become the ground."

Lissy laid a hand on her cousin's arm. "I'll stay with you, Olivia. Let the others go. They'll move faster through the jungle with fewer people."

Olivia started to nod, but feeling another wave of nausea pulse through her head, thought better of it. She grabbed Cagney's water glass and guzzled the contents. The pain radiated across her forehead and she grimaced. "All right. But don't take any chances."

The cousins went to their room. Cagney, Aidan and Tess applied mosquito repellent. Cagney slung her camera around her neck and packed a flashlight into her daypack. Olivia handed Aidan her Swiss Army knife and he added it to the bag along with several bottles of water. Tess finished it off with three fluffy pink sweaters and a large bag of candy.

Aidan slung the bag over his shoulder and approached the door. "Remember, if we're not home by dark, send the cavalry."

22

Operation Golden Llama

The three cousins hurried through the elegant lobby.

Cagney nodded towards the reception desk. "There's Octavio."

Tess wrinkled her nose. "My mittens have a feeling he doesn't trust us."

"You guys go look at guidebooks. I'll go ask for the map." Aidan strode towards the pompous receptionist.

"Hi," said Aidan.

Octavio stood behind the desk, once again bouncing lightly on his toes. He stared at Aidan and gave a lopsided smile.

"Ah, if it's not young Mr. Smith-Puddleton."

Aidan grinned. "That's me."

"And how is your grandma today?"

Aidan shook his head. "We warned her not to put hot sauce on her empanadas. But would she listen? You know what grandmas are like. It could be days 'til she makes it out the bathroom."

Octavio eyed Aidan suspiciously. "I see."

Aidan quickly changed the subject. "Did Gabriela leave anything for me?"

"Señorita Castilla left you this." Octavio reached down and produced an envelope. He dangled it between his fingers. Aidan reached up, but Octavio was too quick and whisked it away. He leaned forward. "Let me warn you, Master Puddleton. I don't trust children. Especially children who have an invisible grandma."

Aidan raised an eyebrow.

"You must admit Mr. Puddleton, your grandma is very mysterious."

Aidan reached up and grabbed the envelope. "You don't know the half of it."

Aidan skidded across the lobby and careened into the small gift shop. "I've got it," he panted. "But we've got to be careful. For once your mittens are right, Tess; he doesn't trust us at all."

Aidan glanced at his sister and stopped. Cagney had a large uncharacteristic smile on her face and something else. "Cagney, what are you wearing?"

Cagney tilted her chin and tossed back her frizzy hair. On the end of her nose was the most humongous pair of sunglasses Aidan had ever seen.

"What about what I'm wearing?" Cagney spun around to inspect her outfit. "You don't like my jeans?"

Aidan sighed. "Not the jeans. The human bug glasses."

"Don't you think they make me look ... well, spy-like?" Cagney turned and admired herself in the mirror.

Aidan shook his head. "We're not on a secret mission you know. It's not like we're about to commence ... oh, I don't know ... Operation Golden Llama."

Tess twirled a mitten and grinned. "But if we *were* on an Operation, I'd definitely vote for it being called Operation Llama. Cuddles would just love that."

Cagney harrumphed. She plucked the glasses off her nose and replaced them on the rack. Fishing in her pocket, she shoved her badly duct-taped glasses onto her nose.

Aidan nodded. He gave Cagney's shoulder a squeeze. "Much better."

"Could we at least synchronize our watches?"

Aidan nodded. He would never in a million years have taken Cagney to be the "spy" type. He pulled back his sleeve and adjusted his watch to match Cagney's – it was easier that way. "Operation Golden Llama officially commences – T minus thirteen hundred hours and counting."

Cagney nodded. "The mission has officially begun."

"Ooh look!" Tess waved towards the lobby. "There they are."

Gabriela and Pietro bustled through the lobby, large packs strapped to their backs.

Aidan restrained Tess and took a deep breath. "Here goes nothing."

Gabriela and Pietro hurried out of the hotel, took a sharp left, and trekked along the narrow path. The cousins followed them through the ruins and down the Inca Trail towards Huayna Picchu. Blending with the tourists, they easily kept out of sight.

"So far so good," said Cagney.

"Yeah, this is a piece of cake," said Tess, reaching into the backpack for her candy.

"This is the easy part," said Aidan. "According to Gabriela they should take a right by that round boulder and then we'll be in the jungle."

Sure enough, as soon as Aidan spoke, Pietro disappeared behind a large rock.

"Let's give them a few minutes and then we'll follow," said Cagney.

"I have a good feeling about this. My pink poncho is giving me good vibes."

Aidan grinned. "Everyone ready?"

"Yes sir." Tess saluted.

Cagney rolled her eyes. "Remember, we have to be quiet."

"Yeah," whispered Tess. "That's the most important thing, right Cagney? Well that, and avoiding poisonous snakes."

The three cousins slipped behind the boulder and headed into the jungle.

"I can see where the brush has been pushed back," said Cagney.

"Yeah, there's the narrow track going down the mountain." Aidan consulted the map. "If we follow it, we should get to a small lake. From there, we circle around Dead—"Aidan's eyes widened. He swallowed hard.

"What's dead?" asked Tess, stretching on her tippy-toes to see the map.

Cagney glared at Aidan. "I'm not circling anything dead, no siree."

Aidan folded the piece of paper and stuffed it in his pocket. "Nope, nothing dead. Just a typo. As I was saying, we circle around the lake before hiking up a small incline. At the top there's a rock that looks like a large eagle. If we climb through the Eye of the Eagle we'll be there. Easy."

"This is so exciting." Tess unwrapped another piece of candy.

Cagney spun around to face her. "Could you crunch a little quieter?"

Tess stopped mid-crunch, her mouth filled with lemon. She looked at Cagney sheepishly. "*Thure.*"

The cousins continued to trek through the jungle. Clambering down the side of the mountain, they pushed through dense foliage until they emerged from the trees. The valley had widened, and to their left a small dark lake snuggled among the greenery. Hugging the lake on its far right side, and towering towards the heavens, lay a wall of sheer rock. As the cousins slowed it became apparent there was a problem. A doozy of a problem.

23

It's a Girl Thing

Cagney jerked to a stop and stared at the water with horror. On the far left of the lake there was a small uneven path rising just inches above the water. The path was about the width of two planks of wood. On one side lay the placid depths of the lake; on the other, a suicidal drop of 2,000 feet. It was nature's idea of the perfect infinity pool, with deadly consequences for anyone without an amazing sense of balance.

Cagney picked up a pebble and inched towards the edge of the cliff. Just being within five feet of the deadly drop made her lightheaded. There was no way she'd be able to walk to the very brink and step onto a ledge no wider than the length of a twelve inch ruler. Aiming the pebble high, she launched it over the mountainside and waited. There was no sound. She turned to Aidan, hand on hip. "This is what you saw on the map, isn't it?"

Aidan shifted his feet and looked down. "Might have been."

"There's got to be another way around."

Aidan shook his head. "I checked. Unfortunately not."

Cagney crossed her arms across her chest. "I can't do it."

"Sure you can, sis."

Aidan grasped Tess' hand. "Come on. Keep hold of me and don't look down."

Tess gulped. "No looking down. That shouldn't be a problem."

Gazing straight ahead and with a firm grip on Tess, Aidan inched his way towards the precipice and stepped gingerly onto the uneven ledge. Turning to face the lake he took a step to his left before helping Tess onto the tiny path.

"You okay?" he asked.

Tess gazed straight ahead. "Not looking down," she whispered.

"Good girl. Now, very slowly."

Step by step the cousins shuffled their way around the lake. Finally they arrived at the other side. Aidan let out a huge sigh and, pulling Tess the last couple of steps, collapsed onto the grass. "We made it."

"We did." Tess nodded towards the other side of the lake. "But she didn't."

Aidan smacked his hand against his head. Cagney was standing frozen halfway along the rim of the pool. Her arms were outstretched as she weaved from side to side. From this angle she looked like an out-of-control tightrope walker. "What are you doing?"

"I think it's more of what she's not doing," said Tess. "And what she's not doing, is coming around the lake."

Aidan got to his feet. "Cagney, come on. Just keep walking."

Cagney slowly shook her head. "Can't. Move."

"Sure you can. You're not going to let a small, insignificant little drop get the better of you, are you?"

Cagney scowled. "I'm stuck." She released her arms from their horizontal position and pointed downwards.

Aidan peered into the distance. He couldn't tell for sure, but it looked like one of Cagney's shoes was missing. "Where's your shoe?" he hissed.

"Back there." Cagney motioned behind her. "It came off."

"Go get it," said Tess.

"But then I'd have to look down."

"Then leave it," said Aidan.

"But then I'll be missing a shoe!"

"Oh for goodness sake." Aidan looked at Tess for support.

Tess shrugged. "It's a girl thing."

Aidan launched himself back onto the ledge and headed towards his sister. Reaching her, he crouched onto his knees. Through Cagney's trembling legs he could see the shoe a pace behind, stuck on a gnarly root.

"Keep still. I'm going to reach around your legs and unhook it."

"You're going to do what?"

"Don't move," said Aidan, as he leaned forward.

The shoe was just out of his grasp. "Shuffle back a bit."

"You said don't move."

"I've changed my mind. Back up."

"Back up?" said Cagney. "It's bad enough going forwards. I'm not going—"

"Do you want the shoe or not?"

Cagney harrumphed and tottered backwards a few inches. Aidan strained forward. The tips of his fingers snagged the heel. "If I could just get a better hold." He wiggled it. "It's coming. I've almost ..." Aidan went quiet. "Oops!"

Cagney dared a glance behind. All she could see was Aidan's outstretched arm. Not a shoe in sight.

Aidan crawled backwards and looked up. "Sorry, sis. It just kind of ... dropped."

Cagney looked down at her shoeless sock and instantly wished she hadn't. Her head started to spin. Her legs went weak. Her stomach did flips. For the first time in her life she understood how Aidan felt when persuaded to board moving objects. A whimper escaped her lips.

"Look up!" cried Aidan. "Look at the sky. Look at the trees. Look at the—"

But it was too late, as Cagney's legs gave way and she collapsed in a sprawling heap on top of him.

"Great!" mumbled Aidan. "Just great."

"Are we there yet?" asked Cagney, groggily.

Aidan raised his head and spat out a blade of grass. "Not quite."

"What am I doing down here?"

"Getting up?" suggested Aidan.

Cagney thought about it. "How about I crawl instead?"

Aidan realized how terrified Cagney must be. "Sounds perfect. Crawl away."

Ten minutes later they reached the other side. They were sweaty and, much to Cagney's disgust, they were filthy, but at least they were across.

"We've got to keep going," said Aidan. "We're going to lose them."

Cagney gave her brother the Look of Death.

"I can see Pietro going up the hill." Tess pointed into the distance.

Aidan peered across the valley. "They're almost at the Eye of the Eagle. Once they go through we can make it up the hill without being seen."

Cagney peeled off a sock and shook several gritty stones onto the grass. "If we have to."

Within seconds, Pietro and Gabriela had disappeared through the hole in the distinctively shaped rock.

"Okay," said Aidan. "Let's go."

Huffing and puffing, the cousins climbed the steep hill. Reaching the top, they scrambled through the hole and glanced around.

Cagney pointed towards a small figure. "There's one of them."

Gabriela was ambling down the mountainside towards several hundred llamas grazing in the valley below.

"But where's Pietro?" asked Aidan.

"Behind you," said a raspy voice.

24

Capture

The cousins froze.

"Er, hello," said Cagney. "We were ... out for a walk."

"Yeah, these jungle treks are the best," said Tess.

"Silence!" Pietro's eyes became slits as he scowled at them.

The cousins huddled together and Tess' knees began to knock. Pietro started towards them and Aidan pushed the girls behind him.

"You!" Pietro pointed at Cagney.

"Me?" squeaked Cagney.

"Come here." Pietro beckoned her with a bony finger.

Stumbling forward, Cagney inched towards the angry man. Pietro bent forward and snatched the camera from around Cagney's neck. "You will come with me."

The cousins did not move.

"Now!" he yelled.

"Perhaps we ought to do as he says," whispered Aidan. "You know, until we come up with another plan."

The three cousins trudged down the mountainside and into the valley. Gabriela was sitting on a rock. She looked up.

"Hi Gab-" started Tess, but she didn't get any further.

Gabriela slid off the rock. Her face was white. Her fingers rolled nervously in her palm. "You were right, Pietro, there was someone following us. But it is only the children. Why do you not let them return to the hotel?"

"No!" seethed Pietro. "They know how to find the dig." He cast a vicious look in their direction. "I don't know what it is about these children, but I don't trust them."

Gabriela stole a glance at the cousins and took a shuddering breath. "But Pietro, they haven't seen anything."

"Puh!" said Pietro. "Lock them in one of the storage huts. I will deal with them later."

Cagney paced back and forth. "This is *not* good."

"Now who's the Queen of Understatement?" said Aidan.

"It'll be okay, right Cagney?" asked Tess.

The cousins had been standing, pacing and generally trapped in a small bare hut for several hours and it was now very dark.

Cagney blew out a long breath. A cloud of mist hovered in the air. She slid down the side of the wall and wrapped her arms around her chilled, hungry body. "I still can't believe Gabriela locked us in here."

"What else could she do?" replied Aidan. "It's not like she had a choice."

"Yeah, that Pietro's mean," said Tess. "I don't think she should date him anymore."

Cagney looked up. "Ya think?"

All afternoon the cousins had watched from a small bared window as hundreds of workers loaded llamas with bulging sacks before leading them down the mountain. The workers repeatedly appeared and disappeared into a cave, but try as they might, none of the cousins could see inside. Dressed in clothes stained with sweat, the workers mainly ignored the three, but occasionally they called out as they trudged back and forth, chattering amongst themselves in a jumble of Spanish.

Twice Gabriela had tried to reach the cousins, but both times Pietro had caught her. The third time, there was a ferocious argument that ended in Pietro pulling Gabriela into the largest of the scattered sheds. She had never reappeared.

"What do you think Pietro's going to do with us?" asked Cagney.

"He'll probably let us go as soon as all the treasure's gone." Aidan tried his best to be far braver than he felt.

But Cagney was worried. She had seen the look of hatred on Pietro's face. Worse still, she had seen the look of fear. A scared man was a dangerous man and there was no telling what he might do.

Aidan secretly agreed with her. He had heard what the workers muttered as they traipsed back and forth and it wasn't good. It wasn't good at all. At first he was certain Gabriela would make sure no harm came to them, but they hadn't seen Gabriela for hours. Maybe there was still a chance of rescue. Aidan sunk onto the dirt floor. Who was he kidding? They were deep in the interior of the Peruvian jungle. It could be months until they were found and they didn't have months.

Tess echoed his thoughts. "But it'll be too late. Stinky Pietro and the treasure will have gone. How's Cagney going to take a picture of the gold if it's not here?"

"Good point." Aidan smiled at his youngest cousin. "Don't worry, Tess. It'll all be fine."

The three cousins had tried to find a way out of their prison, but for a small, dilapidated hut it put up a good fight. Not even Olivia's Swiss Army knife seemed to help. The cousins had quickly realized they were trapped and there was nothing they could do.

Cagney kicked the floor with her one remaining shoe sending up a puff of dust. "This is a disaster."

Tess handed Cagney her bag of candy. None of them had eaten a meal since lunch and the bag was almost empty. "Have another."

Aidan watched a lone mosquito buzz around his feet. The hut contained one chair and several sacks of rice. He eyed a hole in one of the sacks suspiciously. "Do you think there are rats in Peru?"

"You've *got* to be joking." Cagney scooted to the far side of the hut. "Could things get any worse?"

"Don't worry," said Tess. "I'm sure those poisonous snakes have eaten all the rats."

Aidan looked up and grinned. "Yes, sis, apparently things can."

The full moon rose and the three cousins hunkered down on the bare ground.

"We might as well try and get some sleep," said Aidan. "There's nothing else we can do."

"Here, have a woolly sweater." Tess pulled three equally lurid pink sweaters out of the backpack.

Aidan stared. "I am *not* wearing the sparkly one."

Cagney rolled her eyes. "Then it's between the one with the fluffy hood or the one with polka-dots."

"Sometimes it's really hard being the only boy in this family." Aidan grabbed the pink polka-dot sweater and shoved it over his head. "Thanks, Tess," he added.

It was not the most comfortable night's sleep Cagney had ever had. In fact, other than a camping trip to Maine when she was in fourth grade, this had to rate as the worst night of her life. It may have been equally uncomfortable in Maine, but her fear of green flies and moose paled in comparison to her fear of poisonous snakes and rats, not to mention Pietro. Suddenly, she heard a scraping at the door. Cagney stifled a scream and shuffled towards Tess. "Please tell me that's not a rat."

"Who are you calling a rat?"

Aidan jolted awake. Surely that voice was familiar. "Who's there?"

"It's the cavalry," said Olivia.

25

Rescue

The door swung open and Olivia snuck in.

"How did you open the door?" asked Aidan.

"Magic," said Olivia, her dimple deep, her cheeks rosy as she grinned. She reached into her pocket and brought out a key. "Also, this was in the lock."

"Where's Lissy?" asked Aidan.

"Where I should be," Olivia replied, "back at the hotel. We figured one of us needed to stay behind."

Cagney scrambled to her feet and brushed the dirt off her jeans. "But how did you find us?"

Olivia grinned. "Actually, it was easy. I followed Tess' trail of candy wrappers."

Tess beamed. "All part of my master plan."

Cagney frowned and shook her head. "Litterbug!"

"The litterbug saved your behind. Come on; let's get out of here. I've checked all the huts and Pietro and Gabriela are fast asleep in that one over there. They won't hear a thing."

"Wait! I can't leave without my camera. I still need to get those pictures."

Olivia spun around. "What? Are you nuts?"

Cagney crossed her arms over her chest and stomped her one good foot. "I am *not* leaving without my camera."

Olivia looked puzzled. "Do you know you're missing a shoe?"

Tess grabbed her sister's sweatshirt and pulled Olivia down towards her. "We've decided not to talk about it. It's a bit of a sore subject."

"Oh, for heaven's sake." Olivia let out a deep sigh. "Wait right here. I'll get your camera for you."

Olivia moved silently to the hut where Pietro and Gabriela lay sleeping. She opened the door and slipped inside. Through a small window the moonlight illuminated two single beds. They were pushed against opposite walls and between them lay a small bedside table. Olivia stood by the door listening to the gentle rise and fall of Gabriela's breathing and the guzzling snores of Pietro. Finally, her eyes adjusted to the dark and, gazing around the room, she spied the camera. It was hanging from the top of the bed frame, close against the wall, inches away from a shock of blond hair.

Olivia tiptoed across the wooden floor to the top of the bed. She exhaled deeply and leaned across Pietro. Her fingers wiggled inches away from the dangling camera.

"Rats," she murmured under her breath.

Suddenly, the door swung open and in limped Cagney. Pietro let out a humongous, snozzling snore and Olivia froze.

Olivia looked dumbstruck at her cousin. "What are you doing?"

"I was worried about you," whispered Cagney. "Where's the camera?"

Olivia pointed at the wall. "I can't reach it."

"Get on the bedside table."

Olivia nimbly hopped onto the table, and immediately felt something give way beneath her sneakers. "Oopsies!"

"What was that?" asked Cagney.

Olivia cringed. "Pietro's glasses."

Cagney shrugged. "Could happen to anyone. Get the camera."

Olivia stretched over the top of the bed and grabbed the strap. Unhooking it from the bed post, the camera swung in an arc heading straight towards the tip of Pietro's nose. Olivia raised it with a jolt as it swept passed the snoozing man's face.

"About time," said Cagney. "Let's go."

Olivia slid off the table and crept across the hut. She and Cagney slipped through the door and into the night.

"Did you get it?" asked Aidan.

Olivia held up the camera and tossed it to Cagney. "Hang on to it this time, will ya?"

Cagney gave her a withering look. Olivia gave her one back.

"Come on!" Aidan got in between the two girls and pushed them apart. "Let's take those pictures and get out of here."

The cousins rushed past several llamas dozing on the grass and over to a wall of caves etched into the mountainside. They slid to a halt and gazed at several small openings in the rock face.

Olivia stared up at the caves. "So? Which one is it?"

Aidan scratched his head. "Er! I'm not sure."

"What do you mean you're not sure? For goodness' sake guys, what have you been doing all day?"

"Oh, it's been a regular barrel of laughs," replied Cagney.

"About as much fun as the time we all got the flu," said Aidan.

"Except with the flu, we got to watch TV and eat donuts," added Tess.

"You're right," said Cagney. "The flu was much more fun."

"You could at least have figured out which cave the treasure's in," said Olivia, her heel starting to bounce.

"Sorry!" Cagney seethed. "But we were slightly preoccupied with rice-eating rats and poisonous snakes."

"Yeah, sure, the old rat and poisonous snake excuse." Olivia rolled her eyes.

"Cut it out," said Aidan, crossly. "We'll never find the treasure if we stand here arguing."

Cagney nodded. "You're right."

Aidan was stunned. "I am? Well, that's a first."

"There's no point in bickering. We're going to have to look in all the caves until we find something," said Cagney, taking charge.

Olivia stared at the vast array of caves. "It's a good thing Pietro's a heavy sleeper. We're going to be here 'til dawn."

"Good, because it's the early bird who gets the germ," declared Cagney, striding towards the closest opening.

The caves were well-hidden. If the cousins hadn't known they were there they could easily have missed them.

The jungle had done a wonderful job of masking the entrances, thought Aidan, *no wonder no one has ever found them.*

Olivia approached the first cave and pulled one of the humongous green fronds to the side. Tess bounded up behind her. "Does anyone remember if Lissy said Peru had bears?"

Everyone stopped.

Olivia took a deep breath. "I think we're about to find out."

26

Escape

The cousins inched into the first cave and stopped. The cave was cold, damp and very black. Tess felt a shiver through her bones. She slipped her hand into Aidan's and huddled closer.

"What on earth is that noise?" whispered Aidan.

Cagney gulped. "It sounds like a giant bear snoring."

"It sounds inhuman," said Olivia.

"It's a snake!" Cagney leapt backwards landing on Olivia's foot. "It's one of those ferdy things."

Tess frowned. "Actually, it sounds like my tummy."

"Oh, for goodness' sake Tess," snapped Olivia. She pushed Cagney off her foot and flexed her toes. "Please keep your stomach under control?"

Tess scuffed her foot on the floor. "Sorry!"

The cousins stumbled further into the cave.

Aidan peered into the blackness. "It's so dark in here. I can't see a thing."

Cagney slapped her hand on her forehead. "You are *all* idiots! How could you forget we have a flashlight?"

Aidan instinctively reached through the blackness for Olivia and pulled her away from Cagney.

"Thanks!" said Olivia. "Beating up your sister in the dark is not my top priority right now."

Tess let go of Aidan's hand and groping inside the backpack, brought out a large flashlight. She fumbled for the switch and turned it on, illuminating Aidan like a Christmas tree.

Olivia sidled towards her cousin, trying desperately not to laugh. "Aidan. I'm telling you this as a friend."

Aidan looked puzzled. "What?"

Olivia started laughing. "Pink polka dots are *not* your color."

Aidan grabbed the flashlight and aimed its beam into the cave. "Don't even ask."

The beam of light instantly rebounded as the flashlight hit a reflective surface.

Cagney shaded her eyes and squinted into the back of the cave. Her jaw plummeted and her eyes widened. "Wow!"

Olivia shook her head in amazement. "That's stunning."

Tess scooted forward and picked up a sparkling gold necklace. She threw it around her shoulders and beamed. "The lost gold of the Inca."

The cave was crammed to the ceiling with gold, silver and precious stones. Gleaming statues and thousands of pieces of jewelry lay scattered on the cave floor.

Cagney followed her and sunk into a sea of rubies. Scooping up handfuls, she let them drift through her fingers before dropping them into the blood red pool below. "I think we've certainly found the right cave."

"Ya think?" said Olivia.

Aidan nodded in appreciation. "Quick, take some pictures."

Cagney reluctantly put down the rubies and staggered to her feet. She snapped five pictures and nodded. "Okay. That should give Grandma the general idea."

Tess sprawled amongst a sea of emeralds and started waving her arms and legs. "Look," she squealed, "I'm making emerald angels." Her voice was instantly drowned out by the clatter of gold tumbling on top of her. Tess poked her way to the top. She sat up, an ornate headdress perched upon her pigtails, a large, gold object in her hand. "Hey look! It's Cuddles. Just like in the museum."

Aidan grinned. He reached down and hauled Tess up. "Come on Inca Queen. Let's get out of here."

Aidan killed the beam and the cousins stepped out of the cave and into the moonlight.

The four hurried towards the herd of llamas and the steep path leading up the mountain.

"Aaaaaaaaaah," came a strange cry.

"Shh!" Cagney glared at Tess.

Tess shrugged her shoulders. "Wasn't me."

"Aaaaaaaaah!" The strange noise came again.

Cagney clutched Olivia's arm. "It sounds like a werewolf."

Olivia shrugged her off and listened carefully.

"Lissy said nothing about Peru having werewolves," said Tess. "Penguins and giant armadillos, but definitely no werewolves."

"It's the llamas," said Olivia. "They're howling at the moon."

"You know, they're really not as hideous as I once thought." Cagney sidled towards a llama that had just risen to its feet. "In fact–"

Olivia cleared her throat. "Cagney ... back away from the llama."

"What? I was just sayin–"

"Do what she says, Cagney." Aidan took several hurried steps in the opposite direction.

"You're not going to hurt me, are you?" Cagney turned to Tess. "What do you insist on calling them?"

Tess scurried backwards and hid behind Aidan. "Cuddles," she whispered.

"That's right, here little Cuddles." Cagney took another step forward and raised her arm to pet the creature on its nose.

"Oh, that's a big mistake," said Olivia, covering her head.

Instantly, the llama screwed up his face and out of its mouth flew a torrent of gloopy green spit. It was stupendous. It was incredible. It was absolutely hideous as it splattered all over Cagney's horrified face.

Cagney let out a scream, which was quickly stifled as green gunge dribbled into her mouth.

At once the door of Pietro's hut burst open. He rushed into the night, his blond hair glinting in the moonlight, his crushed glasses askew on the end of his nose.

"Quick! Run!" yelled Aidan.

"But he can run faster than me," said Tess.

"Yep, but he can't run faster than a llama," said Olivia.

Cagney stood dumbstruck, rooted to the spot. "If you think I'm getting on one of those smelly, repulsive, inconsiderate–"

Olivia and Aidan glanced at each other. Simultaneously, they each grabbed an arm and tossed Cagney onto the back of the offending llama.

"What do you think you're doing?" screamed Cagney.

Olivia whacked the side of the llama's flank. "Getting you out of here."

Cagney's llama took off like a rocket. The others watched as she bounced along the trail, her legs flailing wildly.

Tess clambered onto another "Giddy up Cuddles!" The llama scrambled to its feet and took off at a trot.

Pietro's footsteps were getting closer. Olivia and Aidan didn't waste any time. They launched themselves at the two nearest llamas and within seconds were careening after the others up the steep mountain path. The llamas were not comfortable to ride, but they were fast. Olivia spurred her llama on.

She out-distanced Aidan, then Tess, and soon bounded behind Cagney.

Within minutes all four had passed the Eye of Eagle and were bumping down towards the lake.

"I don't like this. I don't like it one little bit," screamed Cagney.

"Ah, stop your whining," said Olivia.

"Cuddles won't hurt you. Will you, Cuddles?" shouted Tess.

Cagney spied the water glistening in the distance and the edge of the mountain looming towards her. She glanced down at her shoeless foot and gulped. Shutting her eyes she clung on tighter. "I could care less about Cuddles. I'm just scared of Cuddles falling off the edge of that cliff."

"Cuddles won't fall off the edge," yelled Olivia. "Remember, llamas are one of the most sure-footed animals in the world. Just don't fall off Cuddles."

Cagney let out a scream as, without breaking stride, her llama trotted onto the narrow pathway.

"Do you think she can scream the entire length of the lake?" yelled Tess, as her llama leapt onto the ledge.

Aidan pulled his llama to a stop and watched as each llama easily trotted along the ledge. "I would have thought not, but I think she's proving me wrong."

Aidan nodded with satisfaction, as his cousins arrived safely on the far side of the lake. Instantly they disappeared, consumed by the dense foliage of the jungle. He glanced behind. Pietro had gathered several men and they were not giving up. Spurring his llama on, he took a deep breath and crossed the aptly named Dead Man's Drop.

It seemed like they were riding forever. In the soft light of the moon Tess could see the back of Olivia's llama, but not much more. The llamas had slowed, but now she could hear voices once more behind them.

"Come on, Cuddles," hollered Tess. "You can do it! You can outrun that nasty Pietro!"

Aidan spurred his llama on. "We must be close to the boulder. Come on Cuddles, a little further and we'll be safe."

The llamas once again picked up speed. The cry of a spider monkey echoed along the mountain path and Cagney's llama took off like a bronco at a rodeo.

"Good grief!" yelled Cagney. "Where are the brakes?"

Olivia glanced over. Cagney's llama was heading straight for the boulder at an alarming rate. Urging her llama on, Olivia galloped closer. The path was narrow and it was impossible to get along side.

"Cagney!" Olivia yelled. "You're going to have to jump."

Cagney chanced a quick peek back. Terror engulfed her face. "What?" she cried.

"Jump!" Olivia screamed.

"I can't! I—"

"Just let go!" Olivia shrieked. "Now!"

The boulder was inches away. There was no way the llama could stop in time. Cagney loosened her viselike grip. But she couldn't do it. She closed her eyes and suddenly felt the llama come to a shuddering stop. But she was still moving. She was flying. Through the air. Tumbling over the llama's head. Catapulted forward, she landed hard on her knees. All breath knocked from her lungs. Everything hurt - her knees, her hands and most of all her pride. Slowly she opened an eye. The only thing in front of her was darkness. Cagney opened the other eye and looked down. Nothing.

Cagney gasped. She had landed inches from the precipice. If she leaned forward one single inch she would plummet over the edge. Cagney felt the ground shift below her. Loosened by the impact, several stones around her knees cascaded downwards, tumbling towards the Urubamba River.

Cagney's heart rate rocketed; she let out a whimper and flung herself backwards. *Oh to be back in Texas* she thought. *Nice, flat, boring Texas. Really, there was no way things could get any worse.* Cagney opened her eyes and started to laugh. There and then, she vowed never to complain again as she found herself looking up at the underbelly of a very out-of-breath llama.

Aidan stumbled to his feet, scrabbled forward and heaved Cagney to a standing position. "You okay, sis?"

Cagney pushed a disheveled strand of green hair off her face, shook her head to dislodge the spit in her ears and grimaced. "Do *not* say a word."

Olivia slipped off her llama and glanced behind. The sound of feet tramping through the jungle was not far behind. "Quick, let's get to the hotel, we'll be safe there."

The four hobbled up the path and rounded the corner. The scene below stopped them dead. The moonlight illuminated the ruins like a stage spotlight. They glistened silver in the stillness of the night.

"The tears of the moon," whispered Tess.

"Yeah, whatever!" Cagney pushed past her cousin and headed towards the ruins. "This way."

The four scampered down the mountainside. The footsteps behind them were getting closer.

Cagney glanced over her shoulder. Moonlit shadows were gaining on them. She gulped. "We're never going to make it!"

Olivia seized Cagney by the wrist and pulled her towards the nearest ruin. "Then we'd better hide."

*
*   *
*

27

Tess Saves the Day

The four cousins tumbled down the ruined steps and crouched in the shadows. Everything was quiet except the beating of their hearts.

"I know I wanted adventure," said Aidan, breathing heavily, "but right now I'd settle for watching Mrs. Snoops hang out her incredibly large underwear."

Tess snorted. She clapped a hand over mouth.

"Shh," whispered Cagney. "I hear something."

Footsteps were coming closer. The cousins stared at the open doorway. In the moonlight they could see a pair of boots standing motionless in the doorframe. The boots turned and began to descend the steps. Tess gripped Aidan tightly as the footwear gave way to a pair of knees. One more step and they would be caught. There was nowhere to go. They were trapped.

"Pietro!" The boots stopped. The cousins listened to a jumble of Spanish before Pietro's boots turned and disappeared back up the steps. The cousins listened as the two men's voices faded to nothing.

"Whew!" Tess let out a breath. "That was close."

"We're going to have to get out of here," said Aidan. "If they find us, we're trapped."

"I'll peek outside and see if they're gone." Olivia inched towards the opening and cautiously raised her head. "They're by the Main Plaza. If we hurry we can make it to the hotel."

"Then let's go," said Aidan.

One by one, the cousins shot up the steps.

"Not so fast," said a raspy voice.

Pietro stepped from the shadows.

"Run!" shouted Aidan.

But it was too late. Pietro grasped Tess by the hood of her pink poncho and dragged her towards the sheer drop. In one quick move he hoisted her up and dangled her off the side of the mountain. Olivia stopped and looked back in horror.

"Get off me you big oaf!" yelled Tess, her legs flailing, her arms flapping.

"I *want* that camera," said Pietro, "or I drop her."

Olivia walked slowly towards Pietro. "Put. My. Sister. Down."

Pietro laughed. "I have had enough of you kids. Give me the camera and then you can have your sister."

Cagney looked at the camera dangling around her neck and at her cousin dangling 2,000 feet above the Urubamba River. She sighed.

"For goodness' sake, give him the camera!" yelled Olivia.

Cagney glared at her. "I was *about* to."

Pietro readjusted his grip on Tess' poncho, causing her to drop several inches. Tess let out a scream.

Cagney hastily removed the camera and tossed it to Pietro. "Put her down. It's all yours."

Pietro swung Tess forward, dropped her onto the ground and grabbed the camera. Tess scrambled to her feet and bolted towards the others.

Olivia grabbed her sister and drew her in. "Are you okay?"

Tess was not used to being hugged by Olivia. Normally, if Olivia had Tess this close it was in a headlock.

Tess smiled and hugged her back. "I'm fine. But my poor poncho will never hang the same again."

Pietro opened the camera and checked the flash card. Spying it there, he launched the camera over the side of the mountain, down the rock face to the glistening river below.

Cagney let out an involuntary whimper.

"Now go," said Pietro. "Go tell your tale and see if anyone will believe you. By the time you can convince anyone the Lost Treasure of the Inca has been found, it will be gone. Everyone will think you are foolish children."

Olivia gritted her teeth. "I could push him over the edge right now."

Aidan put his arm through Olivia's and led her away. "You and me both. Come on, he's not worth it."

A whistle blew and Olivia spun around. A flashlight was coming towards them, then another and another. Soon, the whole mountainside was dotted with small beams of light.

"Over there," said a familiar voice. "There they are."

"Lissy!" the cousins yelled together.

Lissy tore through the ruins and flung her arms around each cousin. Finally she pulled herself away from Cagney and sniffed. *What in Great Aunt Maud's name was that smell? And why was Cagney all sticky? Plus she seemed to be missing a shoe.* Glancing at her cousin's face, Lissy made a snap decision and decided this was probably not the best time to ask.

"What are you children doing here in the middle of the night?" said a stern voice.

The familiar outline of Octavio came hurrying into view.

"Oh great," groaned Olivia. "That's all we need."

Octavio plodded towards the cousins and shone his flashlight over their faces.

Tess waved at him before turning her attention to Lissy. "Ooh guess what?" she said, leaping up and down. "We found the Lost Treasure of the Inca."

Octavio shone his torch into Tess' face and laughed. "That's what they all say."

Tess' face fell.

"But we did find it," said Aidan, defiantly. "And we had pictures to prove it, but now they're gone."

Cagney gulped and held in a sob.

Tess moved towards Cagney, slipped her small hand into her cousin's much larger, stickier one and gave it a squeeze. "And Pietro was going to steal it and not even tell anyone he'd found it," explained Tess. "He is *not* a very nice man."

"That is a very serious thing to say about a well-respected archaeologist." Octavio's eyes were bulging. Every vein on his neck looked ready to pop. "Stop this immediately. You have no proof." Octavio turned towards Pietro and shook his head. "I most sincerely apologize, Señor Ponti."

Pietro shrugged his shoulders. "That's okay, Octavio. They are only silly children. I found them playing on the ruins and now they are trying to get out of trouble."

"But we do have proof," said Tess.

Pietro started towards her, but Tess was too fast for him. Bounding towards Octavio, Tess reached into her poncho and dropped a solid gold llama into the astonished man's hand.

28

All is Revealed

The cousins sat in the restaurant of the Cloud Hotel wrapped in red blankets and sipping hot chocolate dusted with chili powder. Octavio and the security guards had arrested Pietro and his men and were now waiting to hear the cousins' story. Lissy settled in her blanket and began to explain.

"Once it got dark, Olivia and I got worried. We decided it would be silly for both of us to follow you. If anything happened there would be no one left."

"So, I went to where I knew the trail started," said Olivia, "and illuminated by the light of the moon was a candy wrapper. It was like following Hansel and Gretel."

"But when Olivia had been gone several hours, I got really nervous," continued Lissy. "I came to the lobby and bumped into Octavio. I was so worried I told him you were lost in the jungle and he had to help find you."

Aidan nodded. "You did great, Lissy. That was really smart."

"We had just started walking across the ruins when we heard you." Lissy's voice sunk to a whisper. "Octavio was furious thinking you were playing on the ruins at night."

"Of course, when you placed a solid gold llama in my hands, things changed." Octavio's lopsided grin broke into a laugh. "Now, if only we could find the dig and the rest of the treasure."

"That's easy." Olivia grinned. "Just follow the empty candy wrappers."

The door to the restaurant burst open and Gabriela swept in.

Tess jumped up and flew to her arms. Gabriela scooped down and grasped Tess in a bear hug. She brushed away a tear. "You are safe. I was so worried."

Tess led Gabriela across the restaurant. Gabriela sunk onto a chair and placed her shaking hands onto the table.

Tess pushed her hot chocolate towards her and grinned. "Drink this. Hot chocolate makes everything better."

Gabriela took a large gulp and smiled weakly. "I am so sorry I could not help you. After Pietro made me lock you in that horrible place we had a huge argument. He was hysterical and would not listen to reason. When I told him he was being ridiculous and I was going to let you go, he dragged me to his hut and locked the door himself. I am so sorry I could do nothing to help you. Then, when you escaped, one of Pietro's men tied me to a chair."

"How did you get away?" asked Cagney.

"With difficulty." Gabriela wrapped a hand around a swollen wrist and rubbed it. She frowned, her eyes searching the restaurant.

Olivia's gaze fell on Gabriela. She swallowed hard. "I'm sorry, Gabriela. When Tess, and the others didn't come back. Well, I ..."

Gabriela smiled. "You thought I might have something to do with it?"

Olivia nodded.

"You are a very loyal friend to have, Olivia. You must have been so scared. I am not surprised. Do not worry. I might have thought the same myself. The more important issue is what has happened to Pietro?"

Aidan readjusted the blanket to hide all traces of pink polka-dots before answering. "He's been arrested."

Gabriela let out a breath she didn't know she was holding. "Oh, thank goodness."

"But the treasure?" asked Cagney. "Is it gone?"

Gabriela nodded. "By the time I untied myself all the llamas had been led down the mountain. The cave was empty."

"Ooh! That's dreadful," cried Tess.

"Do you know where they were going?" asked Olivia.

Gabriela shook her head. "Pietro didn't trust me; he told me nothing. Only Pietro and his band of workers knew where they were headed. The men were talking about it all day. Unfortunately every time I came near, they would stop."

Cagney shivered. "Every time they passed the hut, they shouted something in the window. It was horrible."

Octavio thumped his fist on the table. "If only you knew what they were saying. What a shame you do not speak Spanish."

A smile broke across Olivia's face. She caught Lissy's eye and they grinned.

Tess looked at Aidan with pride. "But Aidan does speak Spanish. He taught himself with his *Spanish for the Seriously Stupid* book."

Octavio reached out and grasped Aidan's hand. "Do you have any idea where they are going, boy?"

Aidan smiled. "I know exactly where they're going."

Cagney choked on her drink. "What?"

Everyone grew silent waiting for the revelation. Aidan took a long sip of hot chocolate and gazed shyly at Gabriela.

Cagney snapped her fingers in front of her brother's face. "Earth to Aidan."

Aidan came back to reality with a jolt. He looked at his shoes and blushed. "Er. Yeah. I heard the workers talking about it when they were going back and forth to the cave."

"Sooo? Where are they taking the treasure?" asked Cagney.

Aidan grinned. "To Bolivia, across the water. Apparently, there really *is* a Lake Titicaca."

Octavio's chair scraped back. He stood and motioned to the security guards. "Get word to the border. We can still stop them."

The next day the cousins strolled through the ruins with Gabriela one last time.

Olivia watched the llamas nibble at the grass. "Maybe I don't want a llama as a pet. They weren't the most comfortable ride."

Cagney rubbed her rump and laughed. "They certainly weren't. But you were right: Cuddles sure knew how to get up a mountain. It was the stopping part he had a bit of trouble with."

"What time are we returning to Lima?" asked Aidan.

"The bus will leave in half an hour," replied Gabriela.

"And you're sure Grandma says it's okay for us to leave?" asked Lissy.

"Absolutely," said Gabriela. "I spoke to her an hour ago. She thinks under the circumstances it might be best."

"But where is Grandma?" asked Aidan.

Gabriela drew Aidan towards her. "Currently she is in Bolivia, near a very famous lake."

Tess' eyes opened like a bush baby's. "Grandma went to Lake Titicaca?"

"Cool. Grandma caught the bad guys," said Aidan, scarlet once more.

Olivia frowned. "What is she up to?"

"I think I will leave those questions for your grandma to answer."

"She's definitely not the boring grandma we thought she was," said Cagney.

"Your grandma is a very special person. She is very proud of you."

"What do you mean by proud?" asked Lissy. "Are you saying she knows what we did?"

"When she phoned this morning we had a long chat and I told her everything."

Lissy clapped her hands over her eyes. "Now we're for it."

Gabriela took Lissy's hands and lowered them. "No, everything is fine. Your grandma is happy the treasure has been found. She wanted more than anyone for the treasure to stay where it belongs."

"She's not mad at us?" asked Tess.

"No. But she did ask me to tell you one thing."

"What?" asked the cousins.

"No matter what you do, do not tell your parents!"

Let's See What You Know

1. What is the Capital of Peru? Hint: it's the City where the cousins first land.

2. How many people live in the friendly Capital?

3. What does indigenous mean?

4. Name three animals you can find in Peru?

5. Name the Mountain range that splits Peru in half?

6. How long is the Mountain range?

7. What are the people called who originally lived in Peru?

8. Who invaded Peru?

9. Do you remember what year they invaded?

10. What is the currency of Peru? Hint: What Tess decided would be better spent on donuts?

11. Name the traditional Peruvian game the Cousins play with Santiago?

12. How many skulls did the Cousins see at the Convent San Francisco?

13. What percentage of the world's butterflies live in Peru?

14. How wide does the Amazon River get and what did scientists find there?

15. What Peruvian instrument do the Cousins hear when they stop for lunch with Lucila?

16. What is the square root of 9,604 and what does this have to do with the story?

17. What is the name of the drawings in the desert that the Cousins fly over?

18. What does Machu Picchu mean and which American politician discovered it?

19. What is the name of the deadly snake that lives in the Peruvian jungle?

20. What is the name of the lake that separates Peru from Bolivia?

Answers

1. The capital of Peru is Lima.

2. Almost eight million people live in Lima.

3. Indigenous means it is native to a particular place.

4. Llamas, penguins, dolphins, chinchillas, tapirs, butterflies and giant armadillos.

5. The mountain range running through Peru is called the Andes.

6. The Andes are 4,500 miles long and meander through seven countries.

7. Inca are the indigenous people of Peru.

8. Peru was invaded by the Spanish led by Francisco Pizarro.

9. The Spanish invaded in 1532.

10. The currency of Peru is Nuevo Soles.

11. Sapo is a traditional Peruvian game.

12   There are 80,000 skulls buried beneath the Convent San Francisco.

13.   Twenty percent of the world's butterflies live in Peru.

14.   The Amazon reaches over a mile wide. A hot pink dolphin was found there.

15.   Panpipes are a traditional Peruvian instrument.

16.   The square root of 9,604 is 98. Lissy mumbles it when awakened by Cagney.

17.   The drawings in the desert are called The Nazca Lines.

18.   Machu Picchu means old mountain. Hiram Bingham discovered it in 1911.

19.   One of the world's deadliest snakes is the fer-de-lance.

20.   The lake that separates Peru from Bolivia is named Lake Titicaca.

Author's Note

Of course, this is a work of fiction, and the lost treasure of the Inca still lies hidden somewhere in South America, most likely far to the north in Ecuador between the Amazon river and the Andes near the Llanganates mountain range.

I will admit, the lost treasure of the Inca fascinates me. It was one of the reasons I set my book in South America; so I could combine two of my favorite things – Machu Picchu and treasure! There are lots of books and websites about the Inca treasure but here is a little of what I learned over the course of my research.

Firstly, this treasure really does exist. Just as you learn in Operation Golden Llama, the treasure was being brought to Peru in return for King Atahualpa's life. Well, we all know that didn't go too well. So what did happen to the treasure?

According to the legend, on hearing of the murder of the King, the gold was buried in Ecuador in a secret cave located in the Llanganates mountains, close to a man-made lake. You'd think it wouldn't be too hard to find, right? But due to the vast and inaccessible terrain, the treasure has remained hidden for almost five hundred years.

You might find this even harder to believe when I tell you there is also a real live treasure map! I mean, this is real Indiana Jones stuff here, friends. Fifty years after the death of the King, a Spaniard named Valverde was reported to have become rich when his Indian bride's family led him to the gold. On his deathbed Valverde decided to draw a treasure map. The map is called *Derrotero de Valverde,* or translated, The Path of Mr. Valverde.

However, the trail went cold for roughly three hundred years, until in 1850 an English botanist, Richard Spruce (honestly, you can't make this stuff up), traveled to Ecuador to gather some seeds (these seeds were later used to produce the antimalarial drug, quinine). When he returned to England he reported that he'd re-discovered the treasure map, plus another map by a man named Guzman.

Treasure seeker, Barth Blake followed up on this discovery and in 1886 traveled to Ecuador. It is widely believed that he is the last person to have found the lost treasure. He reported to have discovered thousands of gold and silver pieces, life-size human figures, animals and flowers all carved from gold. There was also the most incredible jewelry, plus golden vases full of emeralds. The treasure was beyond imagination, intricately carved and boundless. There was so much, Blake wrote "I could not remove it alone, nor could thousands of men."

Blake took only what he could carry and started another journey. Traveling by ship he headed to New York, intent on organizing an expedition to recover the treasure. Unfortunately for him and us (but mostly him), while on board he went missing. It is widely rumored that he was pushed overboard. This was probably not the first death to occur while trying to claim the fortune and it was certainly not the last.

During the five hundred years since the treasure was hidden there have been many expeditions organized intent on finding the gold. Indeed, the Guzman map does lead to mines located in the northern Llanganates mountains. However, due to numerous earthquakes, dense jungle and the change of landscape, the treasure in its entirety has never been found. That said, small objects have washed down stream and been found in remote South American villages, which is a wonderful reminder that the treasure is still there, waiting to be discovered.

Info Researched From

Peru, National Geographic – Anita Croy

Inca Life – David Drew

Machu Picchu – Deborah Kops

Valverde's Gold – Mark Honigsbaum

Discovering Cultures, Peru – Sarah De Capua

The New Encyclopedia of Snakes – Chris Mattison

Nature's Children – Llamas – Amanda Harman

The Inca Empire – Dennis Nishi

Conquistadors – Michael Wood

*

* *

Book Discussion Points

Which of the cousins is your favorite and why?

What do you think Grandma is hiding in the study?

What are your thoughts on Pizarro invading Peru?

Why do you think people from the Nazca civilization carved the Nazca Lines?

How do you think the Inca got the stones to the top of the mountain?

Why do you think Machu Picchu was abandoned?

Do you think the lost treasure of the Inca will ever be found?

Do you think you'd be brave enough to ride a llama?

What would you do if you were being chased?

What secret life do you think Grandma has lead that she's never told the cousins about?

What countries would you like to visit?

Acknowledgments

Thanks go to Hannah H, Ariana D, Sophie F and Hannah J, my very first fans. Claire Fahey who wanted this book published more than me, just so I'd shut up. Carrie Keith who was there from the beginning and my ever patient, incredibly talented critique partners, Lindsey Scheibe and Raynbow Gignilliat.

More thanks to first readers, Holli Green, Carolyn Keith, Anika Kunik and Laura Grovers. Consuelo Montero for everything Spanish. Melissa Fong for all things healthy. Tracie Hill for my Scooby-Doo names and Nikki Loftin for practically everything.

Han and Gee Randhawa for the most beautiful cover art a girl could wish for. Manu Verma for everything web related and Kitty Garza for just being an incredibly supportive friend. My village for keeping me sane and well-loved and Austin SCBWI for encouragement and inspiration.

Ellen Helwig and Stephanie Hudnall for making me realize I should never attempt the placement of a semi-colon without professional help and to Erin Edwards, Deanna Roy and Tosh McIntosh for their invaluable help and advice.

And lastly, thank you to the five cousins, without whom there would be no book.

ABOUT THE AUTHOR

Photo by Dave Wilson

Sam Bond was born in London, raised in Shropshire and has lived all over the world. She currently lives in Austin, TX with two of the five cousins. Operation Golden Llama is her first children's book.

You can find Sam online at:
www.5CousinsAdventures.com
Or on Facebook at 5 Cousins Adventures

If you have enjoyed the first Cousins In Action book, please look out for their next adventure set in the exotic, cricket-obsessed, tiger-populated, elephant-loving country of India.